W9-BBK-743

Catriona had heard all the stories about the elegant, ironic and attractive Marquis of Hampton—his escapades, his amours, his flouting of all the proprieties and rules.

She certainly knew enough about him to know better than to be alone with him without a chaperon.

But Catriona wanted to solve the bewitching and bewildering mystery of love—and the schoolboy kisses that she so far had experienced clearly left something to be desired.

The moment that the Marquis took her in his arms, and she let his lips come down on hers, she discovered how much she had been missing—and how dangerous it was. . . .

THE
REBELLIOUS WARD

SIGNET Regency Romances You'll Enjoy

(0451)

- [ ] **A DOUBLE DECEPTION by Joan Wolf.** (125169—$2.25)*
- [ ] **LORD RICHARD'S DAUGHTER by Joan Wolf.** (123832—$2.25)*
- [ ] **THE AMERICAN DUCHESS by Joan Wolf.** (119185—$2.25)*
- [ ] **A DIFFICULT TRUCE by Joan Wolf.** (099737—$1.95)*
- [ ] **HIS LORDSHIP'S MISTRESS by Joan Wolf.** (114590—$2.25)*
- [ ] **MARGARITA by Joan Wolf.** (115562—$2.25)*
- [ ] **THE SCOTTISH LORD by Joan Wolf.** (112733—$2.25)*
- [ ] **THE COUNTERFEIT COUNTESS by Diana Campbell.**
(126157—$2.25)*
- [ ] **THE RELUCTANT CYPRIAN by Diana Campbell.**
(123387—$2.25)*
- [ ] **A MARRIGE OF INCONVENIENCE by Diana Campbell.**
(118677—$2.25)*
- [ ] **LORD MARGRAVE'S DECEPTION by Diana Campbell.**
(114604—$2.25)*
- [ ] **COME BE MY LOVE by Diana Brown.** (121309—$2.50)*
- [ ] **A DEBT OF HONOR by Diana Brown.** (114175—$2.25)*
- [ ] **ST. MARTIN'S SUMMER by Diana Brown.** (116240—$2.25)*

*Prices slightly higher in Canada

Buy them at your local bookstore or use this convenient coupon for ordering.

THE NEW AMERICAN LIBRARY, INC.,
P.O. Box 999, Bergenfield, New Jersey 07621

Please send me the books I have checked above. I am enclosing $_____
(please add $1.00 to this order to cover postage and handling). Send check
or money order—no cash or C.O.D.'s. Prices and numbers are subject to change
without notice.

Name_____

Address_____

City _____ State _____ Zip Code _____
Allow 4-6 weeks for delivery.
This offer is subject to withdrawal without notice.

The Rebellious Ward

by

Joan Wolf

A SIGNET BOOK

NEW AMERICAN LIBRARY

NAL BOOKS ARE AVAILABLE AT QUANTITY DISCOUNTS WHEN
USED TO PROMOTE PRODUCTS OR SERVICES. FOR INFORMA-
TION PLEASE WRITE TO PREMIUM MARKETING DIVISION, THE
NEW AMERICAN LIBRARY, INC., 1633 BROADWAY, NEW YORK,
NEW YORK 10019.

Copyright © 1984 by Joan Wolf

All rights reserved

SIGNET TRADEMARK REG. U.S. PAT. OFF. AND FOREIGN COUNTRIES
REGISTERED TRADEMARK—MARCA REGISTRADA
HECHO EN CHICAGO, U.S.A.

SIGNET, SIGNET CLASSIC, MENTOR, PLUME, MERIDIAN AND NAL BOOKS
are published by The New American Library, Inc.,
1633 Broadway, New York, New York 10019

First Printing, February, 1984

1 2 3 4 5 6 7 8 9

PRINTED IN THE UNITED STATES OF AMERICA

PROLOGUE

1827

The mightiest space in fortune nature brings
To join like likes, and kiss like native things.
All's Well That Ends Well

Catriona looked up in surprise as her cousin came into the room. She put down her book in pleased welcome and smiled. "George," she said. "How nice to see you." She held out her hand.

George Talbot came across the room to take it. "You're looking very well, Kate. How is the new addition?"

"Very well, thank you. It's nice to have a daughter at last." She gestured him to a chair. "Will you have some tea?"

"No, no, thank you." He sounded unusually abrupt, and she looked at him inquiringly. He caught her gaze and smiled a little ruefully. "Do you know that when you were seventeen I thought it was not possible for anyone to be more beautiful?" He looked from her to the portrait that hung on the far wall and then back to her again. "I was wrong," he said.

"Pooh," she retorted briskly. "Elizabeth is far more beautiful than I. How is she, by the way? And your son?"

"Fine," he answered absently and answered her subsequent questions with only half his attention. It was true, he thought, his wife's oval face and classic lineaments were more beautiful than his cousin's more irregular features. But Catriona had more than beauty. She had an intense kind of magnetism he had never encountered in another woman. He fixed an attentive expression on his face and looked at her, at the magnificent high cheekbones, the brilliant slanting eyes, the generous mouth. Everything about her seemed to say that here was a woman who would go to the whole lengths of heaven or of hell, a woman capable of such abandon, such profound depths of passion . . . His thoughts broke off in some confusion as she finished speaking and looked at him expectantly. He had no idea of what she had just said.

He cleared his throat. "I was going through some of the books at the Hall the other day, Kate," he began, and his voice sounded loud in his own ears.

Her eyes opened widely—a sudden burst of green—and she laughed. "Has the weather reduced you to the bookcase, George? I didn't realize things were quite that desperate."

He smiled a little reluctantly. As she well

knew, he had never been the literary type. "I came across a paper that someone had put into a copy of Cook's *Voyages*." He was refusing to rise to her bait. His face sobered, and he said heavily, "I think you had better look at it."

Catriona reached out to take the paper he was offering her. She smoothed it on her lap and then looked up in bewilderment. "But this is a marriage record," she said.

"Yes. Look at the names."

She did and went suddenly very pale. "Richard Talbot and Flora MacIan." She raised her head and stared at George. "What does this mean?" she almost whispered.

"It means, apparently, that your father and mother were married after all. Look at the date."

"1798," she read.

"And you were born in 1799."

"Yes."

He shrugged. "It seems, Kate, that you are legitimate."

She stared at the paper. "I can't believe it," she said at last very slowly. "It was in a *book*?"

"Yes." He laughed harshly. "Cook's *Voyages*. I've never looked at my own copy. I read the copy at the Castle when I was in school." He moved his feet restlessly on the carpet. "I wonder what Edmund will say."

"Edmund?" She looked at him a little sharply. "What should Edmund have to say about it?"

After all these years her voice still changed when she said his name. George wondered if she realized it. He wondered if her husband did. "I think he might have a great deal to say," George managed to get out.

Catriona rose and walked over to the window, which looked out on the south lawn of the house. Her figure, he noticed, was as lithe and slim as ever despite the three-month-old baby upstairs in the nursery. She stood with her back to him, silent, looking out over the wide expanse of green.

Coming across the grass toward the house was a man accompanied by two little boys. One of the children was riding on his shoulders while the other trotted beside him. They all looked very muddy. They were laughing. Then, as if he sensed he was being watched, the man looked up and saw her at the window. With the laughter still vivid on his face he pointed her out to the children, both of whom waved vigorously.

Catriona waved back to her husband and her sons, then slowly turned back to face her cousin. She glanced down at the paper in her hand. It couldn't make any difference now, she thought. But once . . . God, how important it would have been to her ten years ago.

"It can't matter now," Catriona said to George. "To Edmund or to—anyone else."

"I think perhaps it might," George replied grimly.

"Don't look so upset," she said softly. "How on earth do you think it came to be in Captain Cook's *Voyages?*"

"Someone put it there," said George.

Catriona looked puzzled. "Put it there?" she repeated absently, her mind clearly elsewhere.

He changed the subject. "Who was that on the lawn just now?"

"The boys and their father. They all looked extremely disreputable." Catriona sighed. "Do you know, George, I still can't believe that Diccon has gone away to school! I miss him terribly."

"You can't keep your sons children forever," said George.

"I suppose not." She smiled at him. "I have at least one child securely in my nest, though. And it's her teatime. Would you mind if I deserted you for a few minutes?"

"Of course I don't mind," he replied. "Babies come first."

She patted his cheek as she went by his chair, and smiled into his brown eyes. "Don't worry," she said steadily. "It can't make any difference at all—now."

Her daughter was awake and hungry, and as she sat in the peace of her bedroom, with the silky brown head of her nursing baby at her breast, Catriona looked back. Back to the time when that record would have made a difference. Back to the time, nineteen years ago, when she had come to Evesham Castle, the bastard cousin of the duke.

PART ONE
1809—1817

His sole child, my lord; and bequeathed to my
overlooking.

All's Well That Ends Well

Chapter One

Catriona MacIan's grandfather died when she was nine years old. He had been ill for several months, wasting away to a pale shadow of his normal vigorous self. The week before he died he told her she must go after his death to her father's people in England. She had protested tearfully, vigorously, but he had made her promise.

"You will go to this Duke of Burford, Catriona. He is your father's cousin. I have written to him, and he has answered that you are to come. He even sent money for your journey. He will be responsible for you."

"To England! To a Sassenach! I cannot!" she cried passionately.

"You must," he answered sadly. "There is nothing here for you, my child. We are a bro-

ken people, a broken race. I am the last MacIan
chief. Ardnamurchan is ours no longer. Go to
your father's people, my child, so that I can
rest easy about you in my grave."

And she had promised.

Catriona would never forget the day she left
Ardnamurchan. She and Angus MacIan, her
grandfather's loyal retainer, had ridden south
along the road that led from the Point over the
moorlands to Mingary Castle and Kilchoan.
No matter what happens, she thought, this
beauty will always be mine. I shall carry it
always in my heart. Across the ever-changing
sea rose the mountainous islands of the Inner
Hebrides, their blue and purple peaks soaring
majestically out of the foam. To the north lay
Moidart and the lovely bay of Loch Shiel, where
Prince Charles Edward Stuart had landed over
fifty years ago to bring ruin on Scotland.

And on the MacIans as well. Her grandfather,
a boy of fifteen, had gone out for the Prince, as
had his father and all the MacIan clan. As she
rode toward England, Catriona passed Mingary
Castle, symbol of what once had been the power
of her clan. The ancient stronghold of the
MacIans stood on the edge of the shore, looking over to the Isle of Mull. It had been built in
the thirteenth century. Grim and gray, it now
stood guard for England over the conquered
territory of Ardnamurchan, that wild, remote
and beautiful peninsula of western Scotland.

The journey south to Oxfordshire was very

long, but they traveled by mailcoach and stayed
in the best of inns. Catriona knew people looked
askance at them: at Angus MacIan, who spoke
no English and slept at night on guard outside
her door; at herself, a wild-looking child, gypsy-
dark and dressed in shabby clothes and an old
plaid. But they had money, thanks to this Sassenach duke, and they were treated with respect.
Catriona held her head with the pride of a
Celtic chieftain and conversed only with Angus in Gaelic.

It was a cool day in early April when the
mailcoach thundered into Burford, its long brass
horn blowing a warning to pedestrians. Catriona
and Angus alighted at the Bull and asked if
there was a conveyance available to take her
to Evesham Castle. The landlord looked skepti-
cally at her shabby clothes and said he didn't
think there was anything free.

Catriona raised her chin. "I am Catriona
MacIan," she announced in the clear, soft English she had been taught by her grandfather.
"My cousin, the Duke of Burford, is expecting
me."

The duke's name proved to be a magic pass-
word; shortly a wagon and driver were found
for them, and Catriona started on the final leg
of her journey.

Her first sight of Evesham Castle staggered
her. She had been expecting a replica of Mingary.
"Why, this isn't a castle at all," she said to
Angus in awed accents. "It's a palace!" And
indeed, the beautiful old house made of lovely

Cotswold stone bore no resemblance at all to the grim gray fortresses that Highlanders knew as castles.

They were admitted to the glorious hall by a startled-looking butler, who told Catriona that the duke was not at home but the duchess was expecting her. She was shown into a magnificent room and told to wait. She was afraid to sit on any of the chairs, so she stood in the middle of the room, her eyes on the door. Angus stood by the window, looking uncomfortable and muttering darkly to himself in Gaelic.

Catriona knew scarcely anything of her father's family. The duke, she had been told, was her father's first cousin. She did not know if he had children of his own.

Then the door opened, and a lady who must be the duchess came in. She was very old but slim and upright. She held out her hands. "Catriona," she said. "My dear child. Welcome to Evesham Castle."

"Thank you," said Catriona a trifle breathlessly, and after a brief pause she went to put her hands in those of the duchess.

"Let me look at you," the duchess said and, keeping the child's hands in hers, walked her to the window. Catriona was uncomfortably aware that her dark hair was tangled and dirty from the long trip. She was afraid her face might not be very clean either. But all the duchess said was, "You have your father's eyes." She smiled at Catriona. "Diccon was my very dear grandson, and you, Catriona, are my great-granddaughter. And I am so pleased to see you here, my dear."

Of all the welcomes Catriona had imagined, this was one she had not anticipated. She looked gravely at the beautiful old lady and said, "You are very kind to have me, ma'am."

"You must call me Grandmama. And I am not kind at all. I am very selfish. You are all that is left to us of Diccon."

Catriona's eyes fell. "I never knew my father," she said in an expressionless voice.

"I know. By the time he arrived home from Scotland he was already very ill. It was pneumonia. He asked for your mother in his delirium, you know, over and over. We did not know who he meant. It was not until many months later that we received the inquiry from the Edinburgh lawyer. We knew, then, who 'Flora' was. But Diccon was dead."

"So was my mother." Catriona was looking with intense concentration at the rug. "She died having me."

"I know." The duchess's voice was very soft. "We were so sorry, Catriona. And we wanted you to come to us then, but your grandfather refused."

Catriona removed her gaze from the rug and looked candidly at her great-grandmother out of the striking green eyes that were her heritage from her father. "I did not expect you to be happy to see me," she said simply.

"Well, we are. Very happy. Edmund in par-

ticular was so pleased to know you would be
coming to us. He and Diccon were very close."

"Who is Edmund?" asked Catriona.

"Why, Edmund is your cousin, my dear,"
said her great-grandmother kindly. "He is the
Duke of Burford."

The days and weeks that followed were very
confusing to Catriona. The splendor of Evesham
Castle overwhelmed her. The only family member in residence beside herself was the duchess,
and to serve them were fifty indoor servants
and at least forty gardeners. The family lived
mainly in one wing of the house, for which
Catriona was profoundly grateful. She found
the immense, elegant, formal rooms of the main
house overpowering.

Catriona herself was assigned a pretty chintz-
covered bedroom in the family wing next to
the schoolroom, and within two weeks the duchess had engaged a governess for her. The governess turned out to be a distant cousin of the
Evesham family who had made an unfortunate
marriage in her youth. Cousin Henrietta had
been left with little money and was very glad
to come to Evesham to look after Catriona. She
was quiet and gentle, and Catriona liked her.
She liked her great-grandmother as well. And
the three cousins who lived nearby at Ripon
Hall.

Ripon Hall was the estate that had belonged
to her father. When he died, it passed to his
younger brother, Frederick Talbot, Catriona's

uncle. Frederick had three children: George, who was twelve, Henry, ten, and Margaret, nine. They were her first cousins, and Catriona liked them very much. At least she liked Henry and Margaret. George was at Eton, and she had not met him yet.

There was another member of her family whom she had not yet met. The duke was at Cambridge and not expected home until June. Catriona had had a very kind letter from him welcoming her, but she felt herself distinctly nervous of meeting him in the flesh. From all the information she had garnered about him she was quite certain that he would not like her. And she had a very lowering feeling that she would not like him.

He was twenty-one years old and he was brilliant. She heard this from her great-grandmother, from Cousin Henrietta, and from her Talbot cousins. He had won every prize at Cambridge there was to win. He was to graduate as Senior Wrangler and Smith's Prizeman. He was a mathematician.

Catriona had learned to read and write. She could add but not multiply. She did not find the lessons Cousin Henrietta set her to be terribly interesting. The duke, she was certain, would be horrified by her ignorance. She had visions of him standing her up and quizzing her and she knew she would die of embarrassment. He probably wore a glass in his eye and looked very solemn all the time. He probably never laughed. Catriona loved to laugh and under the loving care of her great-grandmother was beginning to learn how to be happy again. She did not want to have to adjust to another change in her life. She was not looking forward to the return of her guardian and protector.

Chapter Two

It was a lovely June day when the Duke of Burford returned to Evesham Castle, heaped with all the honors his university could bestow on him. Cousin Henrietta laid out a crisp new dress for Catriona and gave instructions to Jane, one of the maids, to assist her with buttons and with her hair. Henrietta was occupied downstairs with the duchess. Catriona took advantage of her governess's preoccupation and slipped out of the house.

She had a splendid two hours. Catriona had been brought up in the mountains and glens of Ardnamurchan, and her slim, small body was quite astonishingly strong and agile. Oxfordshire had not the wild beauty of Ardnamurchan, but she loved the great beech woods with trees one hundred feet tall, the flat, open downs so ideal for sheep pasture, the fields of barley, wheat, and hay. It was a rich, prosperous landscape, and the families who were the duke's tenants were well-fed, hard-working people who always had time for a word with Catriona. They spoke of the duke with a reverence that made his young cousin distinctly apprehensive.

She was late coming home and as she slipped in at a side door she was caught by the butler. "Here you are, Miss Catriona," he said in stately tones. He surveyed her disapprovingly. "His Grace has been asking for you. He is in the drawing room."

Catriona bit her lip and then tried an ingratiating smile. "Don't you think I ought to change first, Hutchins?"

The butler regarded her disheveled state. The single neat plait that fell down her back when she had left the house had come undone, and her thick hair, which had shone like polished mahogany since the nursery maids had begun relentlessly to wash and brush it, hung in a tangle over her shoulders. Her skirt was muddy and torn, her hands regrettably dirty. Hutchins's mouth twitched, but he said sternly, "Come along, Miss Catriona. You have already kept His Grace waiting for too long."

Catriona sighed and muttered gloomily, "I suppose so," as she preceded the butler down the hall. Behind her back Hutchins's eyes were twinkling. He opened the door to the drawing room, and Catriona walked in.

Her great-grandmother was there and her

uncle Frederick with her cousin Henry and another boy who must be George. There were also a number of people whom she did not know. The center of this gathering was a young man who was standing by the window listening gravely to an elderly stranger.

"Catriona," said her great-grandmother, and all the eyes in the room swung her way. "Where have you been? Your cousin has been waiting to meet you."

"She's been sneaking a holiday," said a beautifully timbred voice that was colored with amusement. "I don't blame you, cousin. Who wants to be indoors on a day like this?" The ducal fingers were extended, and Catriona put her own grubby little paw into his. "How do you do?" said this surprising young man. "I am so pleased you have come to live with us."

"How do you do," said Catriona and stared at him. He stared back, and the amusement spread from his voice to his eyes. They were very large, luminous eyes, of so dark a gray they almost seemed black. His lashes were as long and thick as hers, and his hair was soot-black. He did not wear a glass.

"Well?" he said, and she became aware that she was staring. She flushed and took her hand from his.

"You—you don't look at all like I'd imagined," she said with candor.

Edmund's amusement deepened. "What did you think I'd look like?"

"Well," said Catriona doubtfully, "I'd heard you were a very great scholar."

The gray eyes danced. "And you were afraid I'd be stuffy."

Catriona's own eyes began to sparkle. "Well, Grandmama did say . . ."

Two winged black brows rose. "What kind of impression have you been giving Catriona, Grandmama?" he asked the duchess.

His grandmother chuckled. "The child has been thoroughly regaled with a history of your prizes, my dear. I had no idea she was intimidated."

The duke looked appraisingly at Catriona's face. "I don't think anyone could intimidate a girl with cheekbones like those," he said objectively.

She grinned, an urchin's grin, white teeth flashing in her olive-toned face. "You'd be surprised," she said.

"I already am," he answered and infectiously, charmingly he smiled back. "I think I am going to like having a cousin Catriona," he said. And Catriona laughed.

Everything in the house changed once Edmund was home. All of a sudden the various and complicated doings of the household had a focal point; Evesham Castle had a master once more. And there was no doubt at all in anyone's mind that this young man was indeed the master. Technically he had only reached his majority a few months earlier, but in actuality he had been making his own decisions since his father's death had left him, at age seventeen, the duke. His Uncle Henry had never been more than a nominal trustee.

The estate of Evesham Castle covered 30,000 acres of woods and 15,000 acres of farm and pasture land, half of which was rented to farmers. The duke's own farms grew barley, wheat, and hay. He had two hundred milk cows and several herds of sheep. An enormous number of people depended upon him, in one way or another, for their livelihood. He had great responsibilities and he discharged them meticulously. It was not long before Catriona decided he was like a great clan chieftain of the old days before Culloden.

Catriona was blessed with a naturally joyous spirit and had all the adaptability of a young child. She had been sure she would hate England and had been determined to have nothing to do with the Sassenach foreigners. But as time went on she discovered that the Sassenach were just people, just like Angus and Donal Og and Mairead Cameron at home. Everyone was most wonderfully kind to her. And the kindest one of all, to her mind, was her cousin the duke. He was such a grand and important person, yet he went out of his way to become acquainted with her and be her friend.

He made the first overture a few days after his return home. The day was cloudy and overcast, and Catriona escaped from the schoolroom with a fishing pole and made her way to the lake. She was sitting on a rock, happily fishing, when the sound of a branch being trodden on caused her to look around. It was Edmund. He was wearing a well-worn shooting jacket and old buckskins, and in his hand he held a pole that was the twin of hers.

"I decided to play truant too," he said. "Do you mind?"

"Of course not. How did you know I was here?" she asked curiously.

"I saw you running across the lawn." He came to sit beside her. "You run like a deer," he added.

"I know," returned Catriona with pride. "I could beat all the boys in Ardnamurchan."

He laughed and, instead of putting his line into the water, he turned to look at her. "Are you happy here at Evesham, Catriona?" he asked.

She leaned her chin on her hand and stared into the lake water. "Yes, I am. I didn't expect to be. I didn't *want* to be. But"—she shook her head in bewilderment—"I am. I miss Ardnamurchan, of course. It is the most beautiful place in all the world. But it wouldn't be the same without my grandfather. And it is nice to have a family." She looked at him. "Everyone has been very good to me. You must have loved my father very much."

"We did," he answered gravely. "There was no one like Diccon." He reached out and tilted up her chin so that he could look into her face.

"You have his color eyes. And you have his love for people as well, I think. It didn't seem possible that he could die. He was the best person I've ever known."

"How old was he?" she asked curiously.

"He was twenty-two. Just out of Cambridge. He and a friend had gone on a walking tour of Scotland, which is how he came to meet your mother. I am morally certain, Catriona, that he never meant to desert your mother. By the time he got home, however, he was very ill."

"Yes," said Catriona in a low voice. "Grandmama told me."

"He was my first cousin," said Edmund, "and eleven years older than I. But he was like a brother to me. I missed him very much." He added quietly, "I still do."

He put his line into the water, and they fished together for a while in companionable silence. Catriona got a fish on her line and after she had landed him with casual expertise she said, "John said he would teach me to ride if it was all right with Cousin Henrietta. But she said she would have to ask you. Has she talked to you yet?"

Edmund frowned. "Who is John?"

She looked at him in surprise. "Why, he is one of the head grooms. He answers all my questions and is one of my best friends. Please do say I may learn." She didn't know what to call him and so studiously refrained from calling him anything at all.

"Have you never ridden?" he asked in surprise.

"No. But I should so love to learn." She looked at him hopefully.

"Of course you must learn to ride," he said decisively, and her whole face lit up. "And never mind this John," he went on, "*I* will teach you. That way I'll know you've learned properly."

"Oh," she said, as if he had given her some fabulous present, "that would be excellent! Thank you!"

"Thank you, Edmund," he said.

She grinned. "Thank you—Edmund."

Chapter Three

The following year Frederick Talbot died, and Ripon Hall passed to his eldest son, George. George was still at Eton, however, as was Henry, and Edmund was named guardian of all three Talbot children. Margaret, the youngest, came to live at Evesham Castle to be brought up with Catriona. Edmund engaged an agent to look after the estate for George, and both boys spent their holidays at Evesham as well.

It was a noisy schoolroom group, and Catriona and George were the leaders. During the long summer holidays they were always out on the downs, either with the horses or the dogs, or climbing trees and building forts in the woods. All the children, but particularly Catriona, were a familiar sight on the farms and in the stable. Edmund had given Catriona a beautiful chestnut pony whom she loved passionately, and every chance she got she would be out on Caprice, cantering and galloping along the fifty miles of rides that Edmund's great-grandfather had laid out through the 30,000 acres of his woods.

During the winter, while the boys were in school, Catriona and Margaret studied as well. Though Catriona dutifully fulfilled the tasks Cousin Henrietta set her, there was only one subject that inspired real interest in her: astronomy.

It began when she learned that Edmund was being awarded the Copley Medal by the Royal Society. According to Cousin Henrietta, this was an unprecedented honor for so young a man, and Catriona was intensely curious as to what it was all about. And so she asked him.

It was a winter's afternoon, and she had accompanied him on a ride to visit two of his tenants. Edmund had been greeted like royalty, Catriona like an old friend. She knew all the children, Edmund noted. She even knew the names of the dogs.

When his business was finished, the duke and his cousin started back toward Evesham. It was getting dark; the early-December days were very short.

"Edmund," said Catriona suddenly, "what is this Copley medal you received last month?"

"It's an award for scientific discovery," he answered tranquilly.

"But what did you *discover?*"

"I discovered a method for tracking the orbits of comets."

"Comets," she repeated blankly. "Do you mean the things that streak through the sky?"

"Yes," he answered, amusement in his voice. "That is precisely what I mean."

"Do they have orbits?" she asked with interest.

"They do. But they have always been a great puzzlement to astronomers. It occurred to me that by using a certain mathematical formula one ought to be able to determine the whereabouts of a comet when it is not visible in the sky."

"And you did that?"

"Yes. It has proved quite satisfactory, I think."

She looked at him wonderingly. "Have you ever looked through a telescope?"

"Many times. Cambridge has a famous observatory."

Catriona's eyes were shining. "I should love to look through a telescope," she breathed. "I don't find mathematics very interesting, but the stars . . ."

He looked for a minute at her face as they rode through the deepening dusk. "I'll take you over to Oxford to their observatory one night," he offered.

Her green eyes flashed at him. "Will you, Edmund? Really? Do you promise?"

He laughed. "I promise."

"When?"

"You do pin one to the wall, don't you?" he complained good-humoredly.

Her face fell. "You were just being polite."

"I was being polite," he returned imperturbably. "I am always polite. But I meant what I said. We'll go one night next week, before the Christmas crowd descends upon us."

"I can't wait," said Catriona.

"You will have to," replied her unruffled cousin.

He was as good as his word, and the following week, after an early dinner, the Duke of Burford took his young cousin on a visit to the Oxford Observatory. She was absolutely fascinated. And in listening to Edmund converse with the Observatory director, she felt herself to be frivolous, superficial, fuddled, ignorant, and abysmally young.

"That was wonderful," she said to him as they drove home together in the coach through the cold and starry night. "I wish I could understand more about it."

"If you wish to understand things, you must first apply yourself to your studies," came the cool voice beside her in the dark. "It doesn't seem to me that you have ever exhibited much application, Catriona."

"No," returned Catriona glumly. "I'm afraid I haven't." She heaved a mournful sigh. "It just doesn't seem very interesting, Edmund. I really don't care what King John did to his nobles hundreds of years ago. William Bowty, the blacksmith, is far more interesting."

"I see. And do you feel the same way about geography? You really don't care where India is?" She had recently horrified him by indicating that she thought India was off the coast of China.

She slumped beside him on the seat. His voice was perfectly pleasant, but something about it was making her very uncomfortable. "Mmph," she said.

"I am afraid I did not hear you."

She sat up a little straighter. "I'm sorry, Edmund. I'll try to do better."

"If you will promise me to apply yourself to your studies," he said slowly, "I will teach you a little about astronomy."

"Do you mean that?" she demanded.

"I believe we have been through this before," he complained. "I always mean what I say."

"And I mean what I say," said Catriona stoutly. "I will study like a demon, I promise."

"That's my girl," said her cousin. "It is very important, you know," he went on in hushed accents. "Have I ever told you what happened to the girl who didn't know where India was?"

Catriona's eyes began to shine. "No," she said. She loved Edmund's stories. They were always outrageously inventive and hilariously funny. "Tell me, Edmund, please."

He did, and then Catriona, thinking furiously, told him one about a mad astronomer. By the time the coach pulled to a stop at the front door of Evesham Castle, they were both flushed and weak with laughter. "I love you Edmund," Catriona said and kissed him on the cheek before she went upstairs to bed.

Catriona did pay more attention to Cousin Henrietta, and as she was naturally quick, she was easily able to satisfy that lady's relatively undemanding requests. In return Edmund kept his word as well, and Catriona spent many happy hours with him in the library, listening to his extremely simplified discourse about the solar system and the stars. For her thirteenth birthday he bought her a telescope, which he had mounted at a window on an upper floor. She adored the cold, clear nights when she would stand next to Edmund and gaze at the stars.

All in all, Catriona's life was extremely pleasant. She had a far stronger personality than Cousin Henrietta, and that lady was securely under her thumb. Her great-grandmother loved her very much and thought everything she did was perfect. Margaret looked up to her and tried to imitate her in every possible way. In the duke's absence Catriona was in a fair way to ruling the roost at Evesham Castle.

Edmund spoke to his grandmother about this situation one August when he came home from a stay of some months in London for the season. "You are all of you in danger of spoiling Catriona to death, Grandmama," he said to her sternly after he had been home a week.

"She is simply allowed to go her own way with no one at all to check or to guide her."

"The child hasn't done anything wrong, has she?" his grandmother asked anxiously.

"I suppose you don't call it wrong that she is allowed to run wild all day with no thought to improving her mind or her talents? She spends her time hobnobbing with the stable boys, the farmhands, and the squire's boys. I looked at her schoolwork this morning." He looked very disapproving.

"Henrietta has always told me she is bright."

"She *is* bright, which is why it is a disgrace that she is not being made to perform to her capacity. The sort of thing Henrietta is doing may be very well for Meg, but it won't do for Catriona. She can think rings around Margaret. Around Henrietta too—which is the problem."

"Edmund, my dear," his grandmother said softly, "Catriona is a girl not a boy. It is not necessary for her to be a scholar."

"I don't ask that she be a scholar," he replied evenly. "I do ask that she be given some sense of self-discipline."

The duchess sighed. "I don't know, Edmund. There is something so—shining—about Catriona. She is so joyous. So giving. I've felt twenty years younger since she came to Evesham. She is so full of life, Edmund. How can we confine her to the schoolroom?"

"I understand what you are saying, Grandmama," he said patiently, "but you are doing Catriona a great disservice if you do not set some bounds for her. She will not be a child forever."

"Oh, Edmund," his grandmother said sadly. "I hate to think of her growing up."

"Well, someone has got to think of it," he returned grimly, "and I suppose it's got to be me."

Chapter Four

As he promised, Edmund clamped down on Catriona's freedom. He gave her a list of books to read and he mercilessly quizzed her on each one as she completed it. He insisted that she practice her music. He forced both her and Margaret to speak French with Henrietta.

"Only savages," he told them bitingly, "know no language but their own."

Catriona's life became far more structured when Edmund was at home. He was the only person at Evesham Castle who saw faults in her; certainly he was the only one who told her of them. She ought to have dreaded his being home and been glad when he was away; in fact, the reverse was true. There was nothing she loved more than being with Edmund. She didn't mind if he disciplined her and scolded her and made her use her brain. He could also make her laugh as no one else could. And there was a stability in his nature that gave a sense of security she got from no one else. When Edmund was home, Catriona's world was in place. When he was gone, everything was slightly awry.

He was gone for at least half the year. In April he went up to London for something called "the season," which as far as Catriona could discover was a long series of balls and parties. She thought it sounded marvelous. In the fall he went on a series of visits to other great estates, or he would entertain a house party at Evesham Castle. In the winter he stayed home, looked after the enormous responsibilities of his estates, and hunted. And all year long, whether he was in London or in the country, he was engaged in scientific and mathematical inquiry. There were long periods of time when he was abstracted and difficult to talk to. These were the times when a particular theory or idea was germinating in his brain. Catriona called these periods "the tunnel," because it seemed as if Edmund was far away.

"Edmund's in the tunnel again," she would report to Meg. "He probably won't be hunting tomorrow; he'll be in the library." She knew the signs and she was always right.

Catriona had been allowed to hunt when she turned fourteen and she loved it above everything in the world.

"I was born to hunt!" she announced joyously after her first chase.

Edmund and several other men whose horses were close by looked at her and smiled. It was impossible not to smile at Catriona, at the blazing gaiety in her face, at the sheer happiness in her voice.

"You did splendidly, Kate," said Squire Winthrop. "You put the boys to shame."

"Indeed. Miss MacIan can hunt with us any time," said Mr. Matthews, a young man from the next parish. He looked at her with something in his eyes that Catriona did not recognize.

"Let's get going," said Edmund's suddenly cool voice. "It's getting chilly sitting here." And obediently Catriona had allowed her horse to fall in beside his.

"That Matthews fellow is a bit of a commoner," Edmund said as they rode home together.

"Why do you say that?" asked Catriona, surprised. "I thought he was very nice."

He looked at her in silence for a minute. "Did you?" he said then. And changed the subject of conversation.

When she was fifteen, a traveling company of actors arrived in Burford. They were to perform something called *The Beggar's Opera,* and Catriona was wild to go. The duchess said she could not.

"These traveling shows are not at all the thing, my dear," she said disapprovingly. "And there will be a rowdy crowd in the audience. Wait till you are older, and we'll take you to the play in London."

But Catriona could not wait. George was home from school for the summer holiday, and she teased him into going with her. "Edmund will murder us if he finds out, Kate," George had said at first apprehensively. Although he wouldn't admit it to Catriona, George was a little afraid of the duke.

"Pooh," retorted Catriona. "He won't find out. Henry and Margaret will tell a story for us." Catriona was ruthless about dragging her satellites into her plans.

"All right," George had finally agreed, lured on by the sparkle in her eyes. "But how are we going to get out?"

"Luke will leave the side door open for us," Catriona said confidently. Luke was one of the footmen who had abetted her on previous occasions. "And John will leave the tack room open. No one will ever know. Won't it be fun?" And against his better judgment George had agreed.

The first part of the evening went exactly as Catriona had predicted. They got out of the house with little difficulty, saddled their horses, and rode safely into Burford. The play was to be given at one of the big inns, the Lamb, and they arrived in time to get a seat. Once they were settled, George turned to look curiously at Catriona. She had tried to make herself look older for the occasion by wearing her hair up instead of in its usual braid. And the new hair style did change her. It emphasized the almost exotic slant of her cat's eyes, the high planes of her cheekbones, the delicate line of her jaw. George stared.

"You look different, Kate," he said uneasily.

She looked pleased. "Do I? Good."

George glanced around. He was evidently not the only man who was interested in Catriona; there were too many pairs of eyes focused on her newly grown-up-looking face. "I think perhaps we should leave," he said nervously.

"Don't be silly," she returned impatiently. "The show is starting."

The show was indeed starting, but as the play went on it became evident that Catriona was the star. At the first intermission a young man, fashionably dressed, came over to her and tried to strike up a conversation. Catriona, incurably friendly, smiled at his sally and said yes, she was enjoying the play.

George, more and more unhappy with the way this adventure was turning out, said loudly, "I say, Kate, I think it's time we were leaving."

"Leaving?" said Catriona blankly. "But the play is only half over."

"Never mind him, sweetheart," said the strange man. "You can stay with me."

Even Catriona recognized the impropriety of this statement. "Of course I can't stay with you," she said in astonishment. "I don't even know you."

"That can be swiftly remedied," the stranger

murmured. "I'll make it well worth your while," he added.

"You swine," shouted George. "Get away from my cousin." He pushed at the stranger's chest.

A very ugly look descended over the other man's face. Catriona grabbed his arm. "Don't you dare touch him!" she cried.

"May I be of service, my lord?" came a deep, rumbly voice, and Mr. Stiles, the owner of the Lamb, was there. He looked from the stranger to Catriona and George. "Miss MacIan! Mr. Talbot!" he said. "What are you doing here?"

Catriona and George exchanged a guilty look and said nothing.

"Where is His Grace?" the rumbly voice went on.

Catriona and George looked at the floor.

"I see," said Mr. Stiles grimly.

"His Grace?" said the stranger in quick alarm.

"These are two young cousins of the Duke of Burford," the innkeeper said disapprovingly. "And I'll wager His Grace has no idea they have stolen into town this evening."

"Burford!" said the young man in a horrified voice. "Good God." He backed away. "Sorry," he stammered. "Made a mistake. I do beg your pardon. . . ." He was gone.

Catriona peeked up at the innkeeper. "You aren't going to give us away to His Grace, are you, Mr. Stiles?"

"That I am, Miss MacIan," the man replied promptly. "In fact, the both of you will come along with me right now. I'll drive you back to the Castle."

"Oh, there's no need for you to do that, Mr. Stiles," George protested. "We have our horses here."

"I will stable your horses overnight at the Lamb," came the inexorable reply. "I have no intention of allowing you two young rascals to ride back to the Castle in the dark. Come along now."

To their mutual dismay, Catriona and George were forced to squeeze onto the front seat of Mr. Stiles's gig and were driven, in ignominy and shame, home to Evesham Castle and the Duke.

Chapter Five

They were put in the morning room while Edmund talked to Mr. Stiles in the library. They sat together on a sofa in miserable silence, looking apprehensively at the door. When finally it opened and their cousin appeared on the threshold, instinctively they moved closer to each other, as if for protection.

"So," said Edmund as he advanced into the room, "you decided to go to the play after all." His tone was calm, even pleasant, but a shiver went through George and his stomach muscles knotted.

"It was my idea, Edmund," said Catriona quickly. "George really did not want to come, but I teased him."

"I see." Edmund looked at George. "You are, I believe, three years older than your cousin."

"Yes, Edmund," said George miserably.

"You knew, I presume, that the Lamb was not at all the sort of place for a young girl."

"Yes, Edmund." George's voice was barely audible.

Edmund then proceeded to inform George exactly what he thought of his character, his conduct, and his intelligence. He did it in the same agreeable manner with which he had first spoken and when he finished George was perilously close to tears.

"Very well," said Edmund at last, "you may go to your room." Then, as Catriona made as if to follow George, he added with dangerous quiet, "Not you, Catriona. I have a few things I wish to say to you first."

Catriona stopped and watched, with envious eyes, George's departure. Biting her lip, she turned to face her cousin.

"Don't you have any conscience at all about whom you drag into your escapades?" asked Edmund. His voice had lost all its cool detachment; it was peremptory, warm, and formidably angry.

Catriona looked at him warily. "I—I didn't think it would be so bad," she faltered.

"You didn't think. That is always the problem, isn't it, Catriona? You don't think. You don't *want* to think. All you want to do is behave like a hoyden and bring disgrace on yourself and on your family."

There was no mistaking the temper in his eyes.

"But Edmund, I didn't know there would be a man there who would behave so badly. It wasn't my fault he was drunk."

"Oh, was he drunk?"

"He must have been," returned Catriona indignantly. "He was going to hit George."

"That man," said Edmund, taking a step closer to her, "was Lord Margate, son of the Earl of Wethersby. He was not drunk. He just mistook you for a common doxy."

Catriona's eyes flew wide open, and color flushed into her cheeks. "But why should he think that?" she demanded.

"Look at you." Edmund's hand came out and ruthlessly plucked a few pins from her hair. He pulled out some hair along with the pins, and Catriona's eyes watered with the sudden pain. "You certainly made every attempt to play the part," he went on, "wearing your hair in that ridiculous fashion, painting your eyes."

"I did not paint my eyes," said Catriona, blinking them vigorously to clear away the tears. Her hair started to tumble about her shoulders. "And I only put my hair up because I was trying to look older."

"Well, you succeeded in looking like a whore," said Edmund very unfairly.

"I did not," Catriona contradicted him bravely if unwisely. "It wasn't my fault if this Lord somebody or other has the deplorable manners to approach a perfectly strange girl with such disgusting thoughts in his mind. I'm glad George pushed him!"

Edmund was furiously angry by now. "And would you have been glad to see George lose a couple of his teeth? Young Margate boxes at Jackson's in London. He is very good."

Catriona's eyes fell before the look in his. "No," she whispered. "I would not like to see George hurt."

"Well, in future, then, you must think of the welfare of others before you embroil them in your own headstrong and ill-advised plans." He sounded utterly disgusted with her. "You may be able to lead George around as if he were your pet dog, but please have the goodness to consider his welfare and reputation, even if you have no regard for your own. That is all I wished to say to you. Good night."

"Edmund . . ." She reached out her hand timidly toward him. He ignored it.

"You may go to your room," he said in a voice that was colder than ice. She turned and fled.

Catriona was miserable for weeks. Edmund had been annoyed with her before, but never had he been so angry. She did everything she could think of to placate him. She read studiously for hours every morning; she practised the piano religiously; she made sure she looked neat and tidy at all times.

It was not a regimen she found it easy to follow, and one day in early September worn out from being so good, Catriona slipped out of the house by herself and went for a walk in the woods. She was several miles from the castle when she heard the whimpering of an animal. Closer investigation showed her a small, shivering puppy on the other side of the stream.

"What's the matter, little one?" she called to it soothingly. "Are you hurt? Let me help you." Still talking, she sat down, took off her shoes, and began to wade across the stream. It came about up to her knees, and she would have managed to stay dry if she hadn't stepped on a slippery rock and fallen. She dropped her shoes. After she had retrieved them, getting even wetter in the process, she made her way to the puppy's side and knelt in the mud beside him. After a minute he let her pick him up. He had an injured paw.

"Poor baby," crooned Catriona, "it will be all right. Don't worry, Catriona has got you. Come on now." Holding the puppy to her breast, she recrossed the stream and, not bothering to put on her sodden shoes, she made her way back to the ride she had been walking along and started toward the Castle. She had been walking five minutes when she heard the sound of hoof-beats drumming on the ground. She turned and saw a beautiful black mare bearing down on her. It was Edmund.

He pulled up as soon as he saw her and stared down at her bedraggled figure. Her feet were bare and filthy, her skirt was soaked, a puppy was chewing on the end of her long, dark braid, and she had mud on her cheek. She looked about ten years old.

"What happened?" he asked, resignation in his voice.

"It's this darling little puppy, Edmund," she said. "I found him in the woods. His paw is hurt. Look." She lifted the dog for his inspection. Her extraordinary green eyes were full of compassion and concern, and Edmund dismounted.

"Come on," he said. "I'll give you a ride home." He noticed for the first time that she was shivering. "Here." He took off his coat and draped it across her shoulders. Then he rolled up the sleeves of his immaculate shirt and, putting his hands about her waist, lifted her effortlessly into the saddle. He got up behind her and took up the reins. The mare, who had sidled at the unfamiliar burden, quieted as soon as she felt the iron grip of his legs.

Catriona felt blissfully happy. She was so close to Edmund that she could feel the beat of his heart against her shoulder. Every movement of his hands on the reins brought into play the muscles of his forearms. The warmth from his coat and his body enveloped her. She heaved a sigh of satisfaction.

"Can't you ever stay clean?" he asked. There was laughter in his voice and an odd, tender note, which had been noticeably absent when he had spoken to her of late. He wasn't angry. Catriona raised her eyes to look at him. She smiled, and her whole face lit up.

"I've been very good," she told him. "I hardly moved for the entire month of August."

"Yes," he said. "I noticed. And I must say I

wondered how long it would last." He took one hand from the reins and lightly touched her cheek. "You've been outdoors sometimes. You're brown as a gypsy."

"I'm always brown," Catriona replied blithely. "Grandmama thinks it's terrible, but there's nothing I can do about it. It's my Celtic blood. The MacIans are all dark. Look." She stretched her arm out so that it lay alongside his. Edmund's forearm was several shades fairer than hers.

Edmund regarded their two arms for a moment in silence. His was fair-skinned, black-haired, and hard as iron. Catriona's was warmly olive in color, delicately boned, and smooth. "Yes," he said, his voice a little gruff. "I see."

"Grandmama is afraid I'm not going to be pretty," Catriona confided. "She thinks I'm too dark and too small and too skinny. I keep hoping I'll start to grow a little. Was my father tall like you, Edmund?"

"Diccon was tall enough."

"But was he six feet like you?"

"No. He was a few inches shorter than I." There was a moment's pause as they came out of the woods and headed up the ride that led to the Castle. "I'm surprised to hear that Grandmama has found anything about you less than ideal. She has always given me the impression that she finds you perfect." His eyes were on the mellow stone of his house.

Catriona shook her head. "Oh, no! I make her laugh, that's all. She likes that." She tipped her head back to look up at her cousin again, her eyes flashing green as she raised her face to his. "But she doesn't disapprove of me as you do," she added.

"I don't disapprove of you, Catriona," he answered, gazing down at her gravely. "But I am responsible for you, and when you do wrong it is my duty to correct you. I do so because I care for you and am concerned for your welfare."

Catriona smiled, not her usual blazing smile but slowly, almost dreamily. "I know," she murmured softly. She leaned her head against his shoulder. "But it makes me so unhappy when you're angry with me," she whispered.

There was a pause. "Well, then," he said, "don't do anything to provoke me." He pulled up the horse. "We're home."

Chapter Six

The following June the Battle of Waterloo was fought, and that August Edmund left for an extended visit to France and Germany. In the isolation caused by the Napoleonic Wars England had slipped far behind the rest of Europe in mathematics, and Edmund had plans to meet with some of the most brilliant and distinguished continental mathematicians of the day.

"He is going first to M. Laplace in France," Catriona informed Frank Winthrop knowledgeably. Frank was the elder son of the local squire, Sir Thomas Winthrop, and had been a friend of Catriona's for years.

"Who is M. Laplace?" asked Frank.

Catriona stared in astonishment. "He is only the greatest mathematician in the world, Frank. He's writing what Edmund says is the definitive book on theoretical astronomy. It's called *Méchanique Céleste*."

"Oh," said Frank blankly.

"What he has done," Catriona explained kindly, "is to show that the Newtonian theory is capable of accounting for the observed motions of the bodies in the solar system."

"I say, Kate," said Frank is great astonishment, "do you really understand all this?"

Catriona shook her head. "No," she said sadly. "I have no head for mathematics, I'm afraid. Edmund says I'm the most relentlessly concrete person he's ever met. But I understand—generally—what the *idea* of Laplace's book is. What he has done is to portray the solar system as a stupendous machine, moving under the influence of immutable laws."

"I tell you what, Kate," Frank said disapprovingly, "you're turning into a scholar."

"Hah," said Catriona mournfully. "There's little chance of that, I'm afraid. I'm a sad disappointment to Edmund."

"I don't see how a man who rides as splendidly as the duke can possibly be interested in mathematics," said Frank. "Why, he's going to miss the hunting season this year."

"I know." Catriona sighed. "It's going to be horribly dull around here without him." They were walking their horses along one of the duke's rides. "Come on," said Catriona suddenly, "I'll race you to the lake!"

"Done," said Frank, and both horses broke

into a canter and then stretched out into full gallop. Catriona won.

Edmund left for France when Catriona was fifteen and was gone for almost a year and a half. They had letters from him from France, from Germany and then—surprisingly—from Russia. Several accounts of his doings appeared in the Philosophical Transactions of the Royal Society, and Catriona read them carefully. She understood very little of what they contained, but they were a link to Edmund, she felt, and so she persevered.

During the time of her cousin's absence Catriona finally began to grow. She added less than two inches to her height, which still left her decidedly on the small side, but at last her figure began to develop. The duchess was relieved to see that her beloved hoyden was turning into a presentable-looking young lady. Catriona's skin was still too dark, but it did make a contrast for her strange light-green eyes. Diccon's eyes had been that color, but his had not had the exotic slant that made Catriona's so disturbing. Nor had his lashes been so outrageously long and dark.

In her heart of hearts the duchess thought Catriona looked foreign. She did not have a drop of English prettiness about her. But she had a lovely figure, her great-grandmother thought loyally, so slender and lithe and sweetly rounded. And she had a smile that would light all of Piccadilly. And the most generous, loving heart in the world. The duchess wouldn't have traded her for all the golden-haired, blue-eyed English girls in London.

The duchess was not the only one to notice the change in Catriona. Both Henry when he came home from Eton and George when he came home from Cambridge looked at her with different eyes. So did the squire's boys, who had been like brothers to her for years.

"You're growing up, Kate," Frank said to her one summer day as they fished by the lake.

"I haven't gotten much taller," Catriona complained. "I was hoping to at least reach the level of Edmund's eyes."

"I like you just the way you are," said Frank, and his voice was suddenly husky. "Have you ever kissed anyone?" he asked tentatively.

Catriona laughed. "Well, I've kissed Grandmama and Edmund, of course."

"That isn't what I meant." Frank leaned a little closer. "I meant—have you ever kissed a boy?"

Catriona shook her head and regarded him speculatively. He was so very familiar to her: the straw-colored hair, the clear blue eyes, the pleasant grin.

"Would you like to try it?" he asked, very low.

"All right," said Catriona, who was always game for a new experience.

Frank moved even closer and then he took

her face between his hands. He bent his head and put his lips on her. Catriona closed her eyes. His mouth was warm on hers, and she found the sensation of being kissed very pleasant. When Frank dropped his hands and sat back she smiled at him.

"That was nice," she said.

Frank's blue eyes darkened. "Kate," he said. "Would you like to try it again?"

Catriona shook her head and stood up. "I've got to get going. Grandmama will be looking for me. She's got someone coming in to teach me to dance. Isn't that fun?"

As Frank swung himself up into his saddle, he reflected that she had sounded as enthusiastic about the dancing lessons as she had about his kiss. He thought she showed a sad lack of discrimination.

Two weeks later George asked if she wanted to go boating with him. Catriona agreed and suggested they include Henry and Margaret in the outing.

"The second boat has a leak," George said hastily. "There's only room for two, I'm afraid."

The duchess and Henrietta made no objection to the expedition. George and Catriona had been companions for years. And so the two cousins set out together for the lake.

It was a warm August day, and the sun beating down on the water made Catriona feel very hot. She unbuttoned the top two buttons of her muslin dress and didn't notice how George stared at her exposed throat.

"You've grown up, Kate," he told her.

Catriona looked surprised. "I suppose I must have. Everyone seems to be remarking on it lately."

"Who has been remarking on it?" he demanded.

"Well you have. And Squire Winthrop. And John. And Frank."

George rowed for a few minutes in silence. "Now that you are growing up," he said finally, "you ought to be careful about who you go about with. Her Grace doesn't seem to keep a very close eye on you."

Catriona looked at him in astonishment. "Don't be ridiculous, George. I've known everyone at Evesham for years."

When they had docked the boat, they sat on the grass to eat the luncheon the cook had packed for them. Catriona's hair was tied on top of her head for coolness, and the ribbon that held it was the same pale-green as her eyes. There was a faint beading of sweat on her thin-boned nose and upper lip.

"Has anyone ever kissed you, Kate?" George asked.

Catriona put down her apple and looked at him. "Yes," she said.

George felt a flash of fierce jealousy. "Who?"

Catriona picked up her apple and took a bite. "Frank," she said. "The other day."

"You see!" he exploded. "Do you understand

now why I warned you before to be careful of who you go about with? That sneaking cur. I'll call him out for this."

Catriona crunched her apple. "Don't be an idiot, George," she said with amusement. "He didn't attack me. He asked if he could kiss me and I said he could. I was curious to see what it would be like."

"You let him . . ." George stared at her. "Do you love him, Kate?" he asked then, very low.

"Of course I love him. He is one of my very best friends. Just as I love you. And Henry, of course, and Martin." Martin was Frank's younger brother.

"Would you kiss me, Kate?" George asked in a trembling voice.

"Why is there all this sudden interest in kissing?" asked Catriona.

"Come on, Kate," said George. "You let Frank."

Catriona put down her apple. "Oh, all right." She held up her face for him.

George's kiss was a little more daring than Frank's. He also put his arms about her. Again Catriona found it to be not an unpleasant experience at all. When he let her go, she reached up and patted his cheek. "Now are you happy?" she asked.

George was staring at her with a very strange look on his face. "Yes," he finally gulped. "Yes, I suppose I am."

"Good. I think it's about time we were getting back. Grandmama will begin to wonder if we've drowned."

They both got into the old gig that George drove.

"I'm almost twenty now," George informed her as they proceeded back toward the castle. "When I'm twenty-one I become my own man, have control of my own money and estate. Edmund won't be my guardian any more."

"I'm certain he will be very happy to continue to advise you, George," Catriona said sympathetically. "I shouldn't worry too much about the responsibility."

"That wasn't what I meant." George was annoyed.

"Oh. I'm sorry. What did you mean?"

"I meant that I would be in a position to get married."

"Married!" Catriona stared at him in astonishment. "You're awfully young to be thinking of getting married, George. Do you know any girls?"

He gave her an odd, slanting look out of his brown eyes. "I know you," he said.

Catriona hooted. "I hope you don't want to marry me!"

"Why not? We've always gotten along, haven't we? I mean, we could do worse than to get riveted one day, don't you think?"

"I think you are talking a great deal of nonsense," Catriona replied vigorously. "We are both of us far too young to be thinking of marriage. It's just plain silly. I'm sure Edmund wouldn't hear of it."

"Is Edmund ever coming back?" George asked after a minute's silence.

"I don't know." Catriona heaved a mournful sigh. "He's been gone for ages and ages. Isn't it just awful without him?"

"Yes," said George with very little enthusiasm. "I suppose so."

Chapter Seven

Edmund returned home the following November. Catriona had been looking for him for days, but the weather was stormy and his boat from France was delayed. She was in the schoolroom with Henrietta and Margaret working on a pair of embroidered slippers she meant to give to Henry for Christmas when a footman came to tell them that His Grace had arrived and was asking for them.

"He's home!" Catriona dropped her embroidery and flew to the door.

"Kate, please wait for me," called Henrietta, to no avail. Catriona was halfway down the stairs and didn't hear her. Henrietta and Margaret followed at a more civilized pace.

The duke was standing by the chimneypiece when Catriona burst into the room.

"Edmund!" she shrieked and flung herself into his arms.

"Catriona!" said the well-remembered voice somewhere next to her ear. He laughed. "Still as sedate as ever, I see."

Catriona's cheek was against his. She could feel the harshness of his beard against her smooth skin. Her full young breasts were crushed against the hardness of his chest. She had a sudden sensation that she would like to stay just like this for the rest of her life. But Edmund's hands were on her shoulders, and he was moving her away from him. "Let me look at you," he said, and his voice now sounded odd and breathless.

Catriona smiled up at him. "Oh, Edmund, I've missed you so. Why did you stay away for so long?" Her eyes devoured his beloved face: the dark-gray eyes, the thin, high-bridged nose, the severely beautiful mouth. No other man in all the world was as handsome as Edmund. She was quite certain of that. "You're wearing your hair longer," she said. "I like it."

"You've changed your hair as well," he replied. His voice had become extremely, consciously steady.

"Yes. Cousin Henrietta said I was too old for plaits anymore."

He was standing only a few inches away, yet suddenly and quite discernably he went away from her. "You've grown up," he said.

Catriona looked at him out of wide, questioning eyes. "Only the outside of me has changed. Inside I'm just the same."

He smiled. "I'm sure you are," he said. He looked across the room. "Meg," he said with great warmth. "How are you, my dear? And you, Henrietta?" He moved away to greet the new arrivals, and Catriona was left, bewildered and forlorn, alone before the chimneypiece.

As the weeks leading to Christmas passed and the household busied itself with the preparations that were necessary for the reception of a very large house party, Edmund's attitude to Catriona remained the same: pleasant, polite, distant. It made Catriona utterly miserable. Clearly she had fallen out of favor with him, but she did not understand why.

Ever since she had come to Evesham Castle at the age of nine, Edmund had been the most important figure in her life. And she had known for many years now that of all his family she was the one dearest to him. She had not deserved his regard; she had often been wild and neglectful, slighting his advice, lazy about her lessons, but still he had loved her. Since childhood he had watched over her and cared for her. It was with her that he had shared all the warmth, the charm, the unexpected humor of his character. She knew a side of him that she thought he had only revealed before to her father. There was a bond between them, strong, steady, constant, the source of all her security and comfort. His going away had not broken it.

But it seemed his coming home had. And for the life of her, Catriona could not understand why.

A few days before Christmas the guests started arriving at Evesham. Since time immemorial every member of the Faversham family who was physically capable had spent the Christmas holiday at the Castle, seat of the head of the family. The whole house was opened up to accommodate them, and numerous friends were invited as well. As all the relatives and friends were also accompanied by personal servants, the great house was filled to capacity. Meals were served in the dining room, the schoolroom, and the nursery. Catriona, because she was not yet officially out, ate in the schoolroom with Margaret, Henry, and the children of their guests. Edmund had decreed that George might dine with the adults. George, however flattered he was by the honor, soon discovered that he would rather eat with the children. There was great merriment in the schoolroom; the dining room in comparison was insufferably dull.

Catriona soon had a circle of admiring young men who followed her, teased her, laughed with her, and admired her. The weather was cold and crisp, the season happy, the hunting splendid, and Catriona's natural spirits reasserted themselves. Her blazing vitality was like a magnet; wherever she was there was laughter.

For Christmas her great-grandmother gave

her a new dress. It was the first really grown-up dress she had ever possessed. It was made of rose-pink muslin, and the shade brought out the rich color in her cheeks and lips. It was cut in a fashionably high-waisted style, and the line only served to emphasize the fullness of her breasts and the slenderness of her waist and hips. There were musicians in attendance one evening, and dancing, and the older members of the schoolroom party were allowed to come down. Catriona wore her hair up and her new dess.

It was a very informal party, and the high spirits of the younger generation soon infected the entire gathering. Catriona danced with all the boys and then with many of their fathers. Someone brought out some mistletoe and hung it up, and George caught Catriona, pulled her under it, and kissed her soundly. There were roars of approval, and Catriona, cheeks scarlet, eyes brilliant, looked around the room, laughing, and saw Edmund. He was not smiling. He met her eyes, and his own were cool and infinitely remote. It was as if someone had thrown a bowl of ice-water in her face.

As the next dance started up, Catriona escaped out the door and walked to the stairs.

"Where are you going?" a familiar voice asked behind her.

Catriona stopped and slowly turned to look at him. "To bed," she answered a little unsteadily.

There was a moment's pause, and then Ed-

mund said, "Come along with me to the library."
Slowly she descended the stairs and accompanied him to the room that had been the scene
of so many happy hours for them both.

Edmund closed the door. Catriona went automatically to sit on the leather sofa, the place
they had always sat, side by side, when he was
teaching her. Edmund did not join her. He
went instead to stand by the chimneypiece.

"Why were you leaving?" he asked calmly.

Catriona stared at her lap. "I don't know,"
she muttered.

"Don't be mulish, Catriona." He was the only
person who never called her Kate.

"I was tired," she said, still staring at her
lap.

"You don't know what the word tired means,"
he replied. There was a pause, and he asked
again, "Why were you leaving?"

She bit her lip. "Because of the way you
looked at me," she finally whispered. "As if—as
if you hated me." There were tears in her eyes,
and she was afraid to raise them for fear they
would spill over. She kept her eyes on her lap.

There was a long silence, and then he came
and sat down, not on the sofa but in a chair
opposite. "I don't hate you, you know that."
His voice sounded weary. "But I am concerned
about you—about what others might say about
you."

Surprise made her look up. "Say about me?"
she echoed in puzzlement.

"You are not a child any longer, Catriona,"

he said sternly. "You are a young lady. And young ladies do not—romp about—as you do."

"But everyone here is my family!" she protested.

"Not everyone. And even family can be disgusted by rowdy and hoydenish behavior."

Disgusted. He had said disgusted. "But everyone *likes* me, Edmund," she said in great bewilderment and hurt. "No one is disgusted."

"They will be if you continue on the path you are traveling." There was a little pulse beating in his right temple. "You should never allow a young man to kiss you like that," he said.

"But that was only George!"

"I don't care who it was." There was a note of temper now in his voice. "You are being frightfully obtuse, Catriona, and you force me to tell you that the circumstances of your parentage make it necessary for you to conduct yourself with even greater discretion than most young girls." Catriona did not answer, only sat and stared at him out of wide, distressed eyes. "You don't want people saying 'Like mother like daughter,' do you?" he concluded very grimly.

It took a minute for his words to register, and when they did Catriona felt as if he had hit her across the face. She went very pale and stared once again at her lap. It was only a blur of pink before her eyes. "No," she whispered. "I wouldn't want that."

"Well, then, you must be more careful." His

voice, hitherto so harsh, took on the tenderness she had once been so familiar with. "I did not mean to spoil your party, Catriona. I am just concerned for you."

"Yes," Catriona got out. "I know." She stood up. "I think I'll go to my room now."

He was frowning very slightly, but she didn't notice; she wasn't looking at him.

After a minute he said, "Very well. Good night, my dear."

"Good night, Edmund." And she fled.

For the first time in her life Catriona began to reflect on the fact that she wasn't quite the same as everyone else she knew. Her parents had not been married. Evidently, if Edmund had felt himself constrained to speak to her on the subject, it was a circumstance that made a difference. She could not forget his words: "Like mother like daughter." Could it possibly be true that he thought she, Catriona, was—loose?

She remembered how he had withdrawn from her when she had thrown herself into his arms when he came home from France. And tonight he had said she should not have allowed George to kiss her. But that hadn't been her fault, she thought in righteous indignation. George had taken her by surprise.

Then she remembered that she had *let* George kiss her once before. And Frank Winthrop too. Huddled in her bed, her head under the covers, she blushed. What would Edmund say if he knew that? He wouldn't like it. She was quite sure of that now. It had all seemed quite harmless at the time, but Catriona had a sudden conviction that it was not harmless. It was not the sort of thing other young girls would do. Margaret, for instance, would never kiss Frank Winthrop. She would have known that instantly if she had thought about it. She had let Frank kiss her and—what seemed even worse to her now as she huddled in misery on her bed—she had enjoyed the kiss. She had enjoyed George's kisses as well. She knew a terrible panicky sensation. Perhaps, she thought in cold terror, perhaps she *was* loose.

She closed her eyes. Dear God, she prayed, help me to be good. Help me to be a proper young lady and not a disgrace to Edmund. Help me to be like Margaret. Amen.

Worn out from emotion, Catriona finally fell asleep.

Chapter Eight

Edmund was not the only member of her family to remark Catriona's extreme popularity that Christmas season. Her great-grandmother noticed as well, and after all the guests had departed, she spoke to her grandson on the subject of Catriona's future.

"Margaret will turn eighteen this January," she began in a roundabout fashion. "In the spring she ought to be given a season."

Edmund took a sip of tea and looked at his grandmother. They had moved back into the family wing of the Castle now that the house party was over, and the duke and duchess were having tea in the comfortable salon they used as an informal drawing room.

"Yes," he said after a minute. "I suppose she must. She's a pretty enough girl. She will have a respectable portion. There should be little trouble in getting her married off." He finished his tea. "You can't possibly undertake to chaperone her, Grandmama. It would be too much. What about Aunt Fanny?"

"Yes," the duchess replied slowly. "Fanny would do it if I asked her. And she was certainly efficient in getting her own girls off. Both of them married after their first season." Frances, Lady Dawley, was the duchess's only daughter and elder sister of the duke's father. "We may need her experience," the duchess went on. "I am not as sanguine about Meg as you are. It didn't seem to me as if she took very well this Christmas. There was a host of boys about the place, but none of them seemed to notice Meg."

"Yes, well, it was rather difficult for her, with Catriona monopolizing the whole crowd of them," Edmund said grimly. He put down his cup.

The duchess sighed. "I am afraid Meg is often overshadowed by Kate. Perhaps I should have done more to prevent it, but Meg has never seemed unhappy. She adores Kate."

"So does everyone else," came the terse reply.

The duchess looked worried. "Edmund, what are we to do about Kate? She will be eighteen in the fall. We must begin to make some provision for her future. Unlike Margaret, Catriona does not have a respectable portion."

Edmund's black brows drew together. He could look very feudal sometimes, his grandmother reflected. "Of course I will settle money on Catriona," he said stiffly. "I have always intended to provide for her."

The duchess smiled. "I thought perhaps you would. Thank you, my dear." She folded her hands in her lap. "What do you think of a match between Kate and Frank Winthrop?"

Edmund looked thunderstruck. "Frank Winthrop?" he echoed.

"Yes. He was here quite frequently this Christmas, and I was watching him. It is obvious that he's in love with Kate, and if we could assure the squire that she had a decent portion, I am quite certain a marriage could be arranged."

"Grandmama, have you run quite mad?" Edmund was astonished and a little impatient. "The Winthrops may be very decent people, but certainly we can do better for Catriona than a bumpkin of a country squire. Frank Winthrop! I doubt he even reads."

"That's unfair, Edmund," the duchess said quietly. "And you are forgetting, I fear, the circumstances of Catriona's birth. Her parents were not married. That may not weigh with us, who love her, but it will weigh with the world, I assure you."

"Nonsense," said Edmund, utterly contradicting his words to Catriona. "She is *my* cousin, *your* great-granddaughter. What else can possibly matter?"

"The fact that she is also a bastard," the duchess said very sadly. "It has not touched her so far; she has no idea that her illegitimacy is a stigma. And I cannot bear to see her hurt, Edmund. If we marry her to Frank, she will always have security and stability. She will be placed in the midst of people who know and love her. She will never be the target of unkind or malicious words. And she will be close by, not lost to us, as she will be if she marries at a great distance."

Edmund rose to his feet and went to stare out the window. "I must confess I find it hard to believe that Catriona is old enough for marriage," he said over his shoulder. "Where have the years gone?"

"Where indeed?" sighed the duchess. "But she has come to the age at which marriage is the only means to settle her. She cannot continue here indefinitely, much as I should like her to. You will be marrying one of these days, my dear, and your wife would not care to have a girl of Catriona's age on her hands. No. We must marry her. It is the only solution."

Edmund continued to look out the window. "Very well, then," he said, and his voice was hard and strangely abrupt, "let her make her come-out with Margaret."

There was a moment's silence. "Think, Edmund," said the duchess finally. "Do you really want to expose Kate to the ugly gossip of the ton?"

"You overestimate the importance of her parentage, Grandmama." He swung around. He looked preoccupied and a little impatient.

"And Frank Winthrop is out of the question," he said. "Will you write to Aunt Fanny or shall I?"

"I will write," replied the duchess quietly.

"I will bear all the expenses." Edmund walked to the door. "For both girls," he added.

"That is generous of you, my dear."

He hesitated and then came back to kiss her cheek. "I'll see you at dinner, Grandmama." She watched him leave with shadowed eyes.

Catriona and Margaret were thrilled when they learned they were to have a London season together. Catriona had long been curious to see what it was that drew Edmund away from Evesham every spring, and Margaret had been thinking for some time about marriage. They were both delighted at the idea of new wardrobes and less than delighted about the idea of being chaperoned by Lady Dawley, who had always impressed them as being haughty and high-handed. But when she came down to Evesham Castle in March to talk to them and to the duchess, she was more accessible and less high in the instep than she had appeared to them previously. She had not been at Evesham for the Christmas house party, as one of her daughters had been lying in, so it had been well over a year since she had seen the girls she was undertaking to sponsor into the ton.

"Margaret should be no problem," she announced to her mother and her nephew as they sat in the drawing room after the girls had gone to bed. "She is a pretty, well-behaved girl, and her family background is perfectly respectable. The Talbots are not noble, but if they were a good enough family for the Duke of Burford to marry into, then they must be considered good enough for anyone."

Edmund raised an eyebrow. "Indeed," he murmured. He sounded amused, and his aunt shot him a quick look. "Being half Talbot myself, I am of course relieved to hear of the family acceptability," he explained placidly.

Lady Dawley continued to look suspicious but she let his remark pass. "I do not say that Margaret may aspire to the hand of a duke, of course," she continued majestically. "She lacks the particular elegance that characterized your mother, Edmund. But she will do well enough for a baron, I should think."

Edmund glanced at his grandmother, and she smothered a smile as she caught sight of the glint in his dark-gray eyes.

"Margaret is a very good child," the duchess said hastily. "She will give you no trouble, Fanny." The duchess clasped her hands in her lap and leaned a little forward. "It is not Meg who concerns me, Fanny. It is Kate. What are her possibilities, considering her background?"

Lady Dawley sighed. "Really, it was very inconsiderate of Diccon to die before he got around to marrying Catriona's mother. It quite complicates matters."

"Yes," the duchess said quietly. "I realize that. What can we hope for?"

"It depends upon her dowry," Lady Dawley replied bluntly. And both ladies looked at Edmund.

He didn't answer Lady Dawley immediately but sat quietly, regarding his polished evening shoe. His Indian-black hair was smoothly brushed, his flawless hands lay lightly clasped on his knee, and his long, dark lashes effectively hid his eyes. No one else in London, his aunt found herself thinking, could match his air of quiet, graceful elegance. It was time he was thinking of getting married. He would be thirty next year. Finally he looked up. His expression was enigmatic. "She will have thirty thousand pounds," he said.

"What!" Lady Dawley felt her jaw drop.

"Edmund!" came the duchess's voice, clashing with her daughter's. It was ten thousand more than Margaret had.

"Thirty thousand pounds," he repeated firmly. "Enough to make her desirable but not enough to attract a fortune hunter. And *I* want to approve the man."

"Well, of course, my dear," the duchess said faintly. With an effort she looked away from him to her daughter. "Well, Fanny?" she said.

"With thirty thousand pounds I can marry her. There are still some families who won't touch her, but thirty thousand will go a long way toward assuring her acceptability. As to her person, I can foresee no major problems.

She isn't pretty—she's far too brown, unfortunately. But she has a great deal of vivacity."

"That's true," the duchess said quickly. "Margaret may be the prettier, but it's Kate who has the personality."

Edmund rose to his feet with characteristic grace. "Catriona is a great deal more than pretty," he told the ladies before him. He looked at his aunt. "You are going to have to watch her like a hawk." His gray eyes swung to his grandmother. "You remember what happened at Christmas, Grandmama."

"She *was* very popular," the duchess said to her daughter.

Edmund gave a harsh laugh. "It's going to be a circus," he said with a note of suppressed savagery. "I have some work to do in the library," he threw over his shoulder, as he walked toward the door. "You ladies can thrash out all the details between you. I only stipulate that you stay at Burford House, Aunt Fanny. I want the girls under my roof. And you may send all the bills to me. Good evening."

"Good evening," replied his aunt rather faintly. "My," she said, turning to her mother after the door closed behind him, "but Edmund is being autocratic."

"He has a very paternal feeling for Kate," said the duchess. "Now, Fanny, about clothes . . ."

PART TWO

1817

It were all one
That I should love a bright particular star
And think to wed it, he is so above me.
All's Well That Ends Well

Chapter Nine

Lady Dawley took the girls to London in April, and they shopped for clothes. Catriona and Margaret were awestruck by the massive additions to their wardrobes she saw fit to purchase for them. There were walking dresses and morning dresses and afternoon dresses and evening dresses, new riding habits, shoes and gloves and hats by the dozen.

"No one will want to marry us," Catriona prophesied to Margaret. "They'll be afraid they can't afford us!"

Margaret giggled. "We shall both have to find a man who is as rich as Edmund." She looked down at her new walking dress. "Do you think this makes me look too tall and thin, Kate?"

Catriona looked uncritically at her cousin.

Margaret's soft brown hair had been cut, and the fashionable shorter style made her brown eyes look larger. Her tall, slender figure was still immature, but she was graceful and held herself proudly. The discipline of Cousin Henrietta had seen to that.

"You look beautiful," Catriona said sincerely. "I only wish I could complain of being too tall." She looked down at her own small person. "Thank heavens narrow skirts are fashionable. They give me a little height. Don't you think this dress is particularly smart?"

Margaret looked at her cousin. "Do you know what I have been thinking all week, Kate, as we've tried on dress after dress after dress?"

Catriona looked up. "No. What?"

"It doesn't matter what you wear, Kate. Somehow one doesn't notice if you are smartly dressed or dowdy. One is aware only of you."

"Oh," said Catriona doubtfully.

Margaret came over and gave her a quick hug. "That was a compliment."

"Oh!" Catriona grinned at her. "Well, if it is true, what a lot of money Edmund has wasted."

Margaret laughed and was about to answer when Cousin Henrietta came in. "You both look very nice," she said approvingly. "Go along now. Lady Dawley is waiting for you."

"Yes, ma'am," the girls chorused and hastened down the stairs.

Lady Dawley had planned a ball to mark the official come-out of Margaret and Catriona, and both the duke and the duchess came up to London a few days before it was to take place. They brought a host of servants with them; both Edmund and his grandmother planned to remain in London throughout the season.

Edmund approved his aunt's decorating arrangements, winced at her choice of guests for the dinner that was to precede the ball, but agreed that people like Lady Sefton and Lady Jersey were important to the girls' future social success.

"And after all, Edmund, that is the point of this whole endeavor, is it not?" Lady Dawley had asked majestically.

"It is indeed, Aunt Fanny," he had sighed. "But the patronesses of Almack's bore me to death."

"I am sure they find you quite as tedious," his aunt snapped back.

He grinned. "Touché."

Lady Dawley looked assessingly at her nephew. She didn't really believe anyone found Edmund tedious. Aside from being the noblest, not to mention the richest, prize on the marriage mart, he was extraordinarily handsome and could charm the moon out of the sky when he exerted himself. So far he had shown no inclination toward marriage. He had had, one heard, several very comfortable arrangements outside marriage, but they did not interest Lady Dawley. His marriage prospects did.

"You will be thirty next year," she said bluntly. "It is time you were setting up your nursery, Edmund. Margaret and Kate are not the only ones whose marriage you ought to be thinking of."

He blinked. "I find this sudden concern with my age very distressing." His voice was soft. "I am not quite in my dotage."

"I did not say you were." That soft voice of Edmund's always made those who knew him wary. "I wish only to point out to you that your heir presently is your cousin, Laurence Faversham."

Edmund's eyes were half veiled by his lashes. "That is a depressing thought," he agreed.

Lady Dawley shuddered. "To think of Laurence Faversham as the next duke!"

"I am not in my grave yet," Edmund said and now he sounded impatient. "You may leave me to fulfill my duty in my own time, Aunt. Your concern is Margaret and Catriona."

Lady Dawley knew when she had reached her limit. "Yes, Edmund. And I think you will be pleased with my arrangements for Wednesday's ball."

Lady Dawley's arrangements were flawless. And she was very pleased with the looks of her protegées on their great night. Margaret wore a dress of white spider gauze over a pale-pink satin slip. Her soft brown eyes were brighter than usual and, she had some color in her usually pale cheeks. Catriona's dress was simpler than Margaret's. It was a primrose muslin that made her olive skin look warmly creamy rather than sallow. She was still too brown, in Lady Dawley's opinion, but there was no denying that her pale eyes were extraordinarily striking against that skin. And her new hairstyle gave her height and drew attention to the beautiful curve of her neck. She was small, but beautifully made. Lady Dawley thought she would do.

The dinner party, which consisted mainly of the ton's more important hostesses and their spouses, went very well. Both Margaret and Catriona had been well trained and were neither unduly forward or shy. As the remainder of the guests began to arrive, Lady Dawley and Edmund stood at the top of the stairs to receive them. It was not until later in the evening that they were able to see what was happening in the ballroom.

They found Catriona dancing with the Marquis of Hampton, one of the most notorious rakes in London. He was unmarried, had first lost and then won a fortune at the gaming table, and did not usually bother with young girls in their first season.

"Christ," said Edmund's voice in his aunt's ear. "What is Catriona doing dancing with *Hampton*?"

"I don't know," replied Lady Dawley in distress.

"What did you invite him for?" Edmund's face, when she glanced at him, was coolly unconcerned. He sounded savage.

"I invited his sister Louisa Hartley. She is

rather a figure in the ton, Edmund, you know that. Hampton escorted her tonight. She said her husband was ill."

The music came to a halt, and Catriona and the Marquis of Hampton began to walk back toward the duchess.

"Excuse me," Edmund muttered and began to walk purposefully in the same direction. In two minutes he had skillfully dispatched the Marquis and with Catriona's hand on his arm was taking the dance floor.

"How the devil did you come to be dancing with Hampton?" he asked her irritably as they waited for the music to start.

"He asked me," she replied simply. "He said his sister was a friend of Aunt Fanny's."

"Well, he is not at all the thing."

"I liked him," said Catriona. "He was telling me about some of the people who are here." She glanced up at him, her eyes brilliant with impish laughter. "Actually, I can see why he might not be quite the thing," she confessed, "but he is awfully funny."

"Doubtless," he replied severely, "but you will not dance with him again. A flirtation with Hampton would be fatal to your reputation."

All the sparkling gaiety left her face. "Yes, Edmund," she said, very low. The music came to an end, and they were immediately approached by the Earl of Wareham.

"I believe this is my dance, Miss MacIan," he

said to her. Then, to Edmund, "You have surprised us all, Burford."

Edmund didn't reply immediately, and Catriona asked, "Why has Edmund surprised you, my lord?"

Both men looked for a minute into her slanting green eyes with their innocent, hidden power. Then Edmund smiled. "He is surprised that I have so grown-up and so lovely a ward," he answered lightly and touched her cheek. Catriona smiled back at him, a dreamy, bewitching smile, as her previous unhappiness fled before his approving words. Edmund stepped back. "I must find your cousin," he said, nodded to Lord Wareham, and left them. A short while later Catriona saw him dancing with Margaret.

The ball was a success. Catriona danced every dance, and if Margaret was not as besieged as her cousin, she was kept quite busy enough. There remained only one more obstacle to be surmounted before Catriona could be counted as successfully launched into the highest and most fashionable circle in London society. First she must have a voucher to Almack's. For Margaret there would be no trouble. But Catriona . . . It was with some apprehension that Lady Dawley tackled Lady Jersey on this subject.

"A voucher for Miss MacIan?" Lady Jersey echoed, her brows contracting slightly. She took her position as arbitress of London's most exclusive social club very seriously. "It would be most irregular, Fanny."

"Yes," said Lady Dawley. "I realize that, Sally. But she is Burford's ward."

"True." Lady Jersey gave her friend a sharp, slanting look. "If I gave Miss MacIan a voucher, could we expect to see Burford accompany her?"

Lady Dawley recognized a bargain when she was offered one. "Of course," she replied promptly. "He will want to keep an eye on both of his cousins."

The two ladies watched the dance floor in silence for a moment. Edmund was dancing with Catriona. "I don't believe Burford has set foot in Almack's in three years," said Lady Jersey. "It is time he was getting married himself. How old is he now?"

"Twenty-nine. And I shouldn't be at all surprised if he wasn't on the look-out for a wife this season—once his obligation to Catriona and Margaret is safely discharged."

"He takes his guardianship seriously, then."

"Yes. One thing one can always say about Burford is that he doesn't shirk his responsibilities."

Lady Jersey looked at Catriona. "It is a great pity she is illegitimate," she murmured. "With those looks and a respectable fortune she could do very well."

"She will have thirty thousand pounds," said Lady Dawley, who thought it was a good idea to clarify this important matter right at the start.

Lady Jersey slowly turned her head to look at her friend. "So," she said and raised an eyebrow.

"Burford had a great regard for Catriona's father. They were reared together."

On the floor the music stopped and a slender, fair-haired man approached Catriona and the duke. They spoke together for a minute, and then Catriona smiled up at her cousin. After a moment the duke left, and Catriona and the blond man took their places on the dance floor.

"The Earl of Wareham," murmured Lady Jersey. "After your nephew he must rank as the biggest catch on the marriage mart."

"Very fastidious, the Warehams," said Lady Dawley.

"Very," replied her friend.

They watched the dancing couple. The young earl's eyes were glued to Catriona's face, and he was smiling.

"With that face, however," murmured the august patroness of Almack's, "anything might happen."

"Catriona's face?" said Lady Dawley in surprise. "Do you think she is pretty, Sally?"

Lady Jersey laughed. "No. She's not pretty. Your other charge is the one who is pretty."

"What then do you mean?"

Lady Jersey watched Catriona for a few more seconds. She turned back to her friend. "What your Catriona has is far more lethal than mere prettiness, my dear. She's got what is needed to drive a man right off his balance." Lady Jersey smiled. "I shall certainly send you vouchers to Almack's, Fanny. I foresee some very amusing evenings in the near future."

Chapter Ten

The vouchers for Almack's duly arrived, and Catriona and Margaret were allowed admittance into that holy of holies, showcase for all the marriageable young ladies in London. They were chaperoned by the Viscountess of Dawley and escorted by the Duke of Burford. After hearing it talked about as the epitome of every girl's dream, Catriona found it sadly disappointing—almost dreary.

"Is this *it*?" she whispered to Edmund as they came into the assembly rooms after giving up their cloaks to Mr. Willis and his minions.

He grinned. "It is."

"But it isn't grand at all."

"No. Lord, here comes Mrs. Drummond Burrell. On your best behavior now, Catriona."

Mrs. Drummond Burrell sailed up to them majestically, and Lady Dawley presented Catriona and Margaret. The patroness barely glanced at the girls; her graciousness was all for the duke. He responded pleasantly, and they all moved further into the room.

"Now, remember," said Lady Dawley in a low voice to the girls, "you may not waltz until one of the patronesses gives her permission."

Catriona's eyes flashed, and Lady Dawley said hastily, "You must not offend Mrs. Drummond Burrell, Kate."

"But what is so wrong about waltzing?" Catriona asked indignantly.

"It is not waltzing that is wrong, it is waltzing without permission." Edmund looked cynical. "Power does terrible things to people."

"Mrs. Drummond Burrell," muttered Catriona. "Huh."

Edmund smiled. "Precisely."

It should have been a very pleasant evening, Mrs. Drummond Burrell notwithstanding. Catriona's hand was solicited for every dance, and Lady Jersey formally presented Lord Wareham to her as a partner for the waltz. Lady Dawley was very pleased with her success, and Margaret danced twice and went for supper with a quiet young man whom she seemed to like very much.

Edmund did not dance with Catriona. He danced instead with a number of young ladies and twice with a tall, blond beauty, who along with Catriona was the undoubted belle of the assembly.

"Who is that dancing with my cousin?" Catriona asked Lord Wareham as they gracefully circled the floor.

Lord Wareham looked. "That is Lady Sophia Heatherstone," he answered readily. "The Earl of Marley's daughter. She was last season's Incomparable." He smiled at Catriona. "I fear this season she will have to give way to a greater claim."

Catriona ignored him and continued to look at Edmund, her brow furrowed. "She's very beautiful," she said at last glumly. "So tall. And blond."

"Come, that's good news," said Lord Wareham playfully. "Do you like blonds, Miss MacIan?"

Catriona looked at last at her fair-haired partner. She raised an eyebrow. "It depends on the blond," she said.

He laughed and swung her in a circle. "We must discuss this further."

"Some other time, my lord," she replied sweetly. "Our dance is ending, and I have promised this next to Mr. Hardy."

She danced with Mr. Hardy and then with several other gentlemen and then with Lord Wareham again. A number of mamas of eligible daughters were looking daggers at her by the end of the evening and Lady Dawley was in high good humor. She talked all the way home in the carriage and so did not notice Catriona's unusual silence.

Edmund did and put a restraining hand on Catriona's arm as she made to follow Lady Dawley upstairs once they had reached Burford House in Grosvenor Square. "I want to talk to Catriona for a moment, Aunt Fanny," he said. "I won't keep her long."

Lady Dawley yawned. "All right, Edmund. Good night. Good night, my dear."

"Good night," answered Catriona in a subdued voice and followed Edmund into the library, where a fire was still burning. "Have I done something wrong?" she asked him.

He looked surprised. "No. Of course not. Sit down, Catriona." He went to a table in the corner and poured himself a glass of wine.

"May I have some, Edmund?" she asked hopefully.

He paused. "Don't dare tell Aunt Fanny I gave you port."

She sat up eagerly. "I won't. I promise." He brought her a glass, and she sipped it cautiously. She closed her eyes and then opened them. "Delicious," she said.

He laughed. "Every other girl in the world would have made a face and called it nasty."

Catriona took another sip. "It isn't nasty at all. I like it."

The smile still lingered on his lips. "I knew you would." He came and sat down across from her. "Did anything happen this evening to upset you, Catriona?"

Her eyes shifted away from his. "Why do you ask?" she parried.

"You've been so quiet. Too quiet." He put his glass down and reached over and grasped her hand. "What was it, sweetheart?"

The endearment brought tears to her eyes. "Ah," she said, thinking quickly, "it was something I overheard at Almack's." She was refusing to look at him. "One of the chaperons—she said that it was disgusting to see a little bastard like me queening it in good society."

Edmund's hand tightened, and he swore under his breath. Her head jerked up in surprise, and he moved from his chair to sit next to her on the sofa.

"She was jealous," he said. "That's why she said that. Her own daughter was probably sitting on a chair all evening watching you."

"But it makes a difference, doesn't it?" Catriona said slowly. "The fact that my mother and father were not married."

"Only to some people," said Edmund and put an arm about her. She pressed her cheek into his shoulder. "It shouldn't," he went on softly. "It has nothing to do with you. And it will never make a difference to anyone who truly loves you. So you must simply learn not to hear remarks such as you overheard this evening."

Catriona didn't move. "Yes, Edmund," she breathed.

"Whenever someone says anything unkind, it is always a good idea to consider the source," he advised. He took his arm away, and Catriona was forced to raise her head. "All right?" he asked gently.

"Yes. Actually, I feel sorry for people like that. It must be frightful to have such a narrow, censorious mind."

He smiled at her. "Unlike you, who likes everybody."

"Well, I do. And I'm used to people liking me back. Mrs. Drummond Burrell didn't like me, though." She grinned at him engagingly. "But my, she certainly liked *you*."

Edmund looked sardonic. "They have been trying to get me to Almack's for ages."

"Why?"

"They want to marry me off, of course. Every woman I know seems to have received a special mission from God lately to arrange my nuptials."

"Oh." Catriona looked impish. "Too bad Mrs. Drummond Burrell is already married. She certainly looked interested in you. If I were Mr. Drummond Burrell, I wouldn't stand next to any open windows."

"Don't be ridiculous," said Edmund.

Catriona jumped up and stood in front of him. "Miss MacIan," she said through her nose, in a very fair imitation of the Almack's patroness. She gazed over his head as if scanning some far horizon.

Edmund chuckled. "Didn't she even look at you?"

"No. Her eyes were all for you. *Your Grace*," she said in a languishing voice, batting her remarkable lashes.

He laughed. "Don't pay any attention to her. I never do."

"Well, she certainly paid attention to you."

He rose to his feet. "Next time you must tell her that the only reason I come to Almack's is to keep an eye on you. Perhaps you will partake of my reflected glory."

Catriona glowed with a light that was all her own. "Is that true? Are you coming just for me?"

"Of course. And it's time you went up to bed."

"But you didn't dance with me," she said as she obediently moved toward the door.

"I didn't want to risk the wrath of your prospective suitors."

"Pooh," said Catriona. "I don't care about *them*." She smiled. "Good night, Edmund."

His face was suddenly grave. "Good night, Catriona."

She went upstairs feeling happier than she had in a very long time.

Chapter Eleven

Several bouquets of flowers arrived for Catriona the day after the Almack's assembly, and one for Margaret from Mr. Frederick Halley, the quiet young man who had danced with her twice the previous evening.

"Who are yours from, Kate?" Margaret asked as she looked at the impressive lineup. Her voice held just the faintest tinge of envy.

"Oh, Mr. Hardy, Mr. Morrison, Lord Wareham, and one or two others." Catriona smiled at Margaret. "I don't need to ask who yours are from, Meg. You only paid attention to *one* young man last night. Is he nice?"

Margaret smiled back. "Yes," she said. "He is. This is his first season, too. He only came down from Cambridge last year. He knows George."

"Does he? That must be why you spent so much time talking to him," Catriona teased.

Margaret flushed. "I only danced with him twice. You danced with Lord Wareham twice. And Mr. Hardy."

"That's different," said Catriona.

"Why?"

Catriona frowned and looked at the sweet face of her cousin. "I don't know," she said at last. "But it is."

"I don't see why."

Catriona looked somber. "It's because you're a better person than I am, Meg. You don't do things on impulse. You—think."

"I think too much sometimes," returned Margaret. "Don't you know how I've always longed to be like you?"

"Like me? But why? You're much prettier than I am, have better manners, do the proper thing. . . ."

"Stop!" Margaret held up her hand. "You make me sound as dull as I am. The truth is that I haven't got the nerve to do the things you do. For example, I should have loved to have seen that play with you and George a few years ago, but I was afraid to risk it."

"Oh, that." Catriona shuddered theatrically. "I wish I hadn't risked it. When I think of how angry Edmund was . . ."

"I could never face Edmund when he gets like that." Margaret's cheeks were pale at the thought. "I shall never forget what he said to

Henry the time he got sent down from Eton. I'd rather be skinned alive than have him speak to me like that. He's so—so quiet. So pleasant. So annihilating."

"Well, he isn't quiet and pleasant when he gets angry at me," Catriona said decidedly. "He is just furious."

"I don't believe I've ever seen Edmund lose his temper," Margaret said slowly.

"Hah," said Catriona. "You've never heard him dressing me down."

"And you don't mind it?" asked Margaret incredulously.

"Of course I mind it." Catriona was very serious now. "I hate it when Edmund is angry with me."

Margaret looked around the flower-filled room. "Well, he can't be angry with you now. You are a Success, Kate. Marriage offers will be pouring in."

"I don't think so." Catriona's gravity lifted and she looked decidedly happier. "Consider my wretched background, Meg. I'm a bastard. I don't think anyone will want to marry me."

Margaret stared at her. "That won't matter, Kate."

"Oh, yes, it will. Edmund said it would last night when he was trying to cheer me up."

"Trying to cheer you up? By telling you no one would want to marry you?"

"Oh, he didn't say that. But he meant it all the same." Catriona grinned at Margaret. "Don't look so upset. I don't at all want to get married. Now I can just have fun and not worry about having to leave Evesham."

"I see," said Margaret blankly.

Catriona proceeded to fulfill her own prophecy and have fun. She went driving in the park with a variety of eligible men. She went to balls and danced with a variety of eligible men. She went to the theater, and between acts her box was filled with a variety of eligible men. Everyone was very nice, she thought. And no one got too close. Lady Dawley and the duke saw to that. So she relaxed and enjoyed herself outrageously.

After their conversation the night of her first Almack's assembly Edmund withdrew from Catriona again. He dutifully escorted her and Margaret to the more important of their engagements and put in an occasional appearance at Almack's, but otherwise appeared preoccupied. Catriona noticed that the light was always on in the library when she returned home late at night and assumed he was working on a new mathematics formula.

Consequently the conversation between her great-grandmother and Lady Dawley that she overheard took her completely by surprise. She was sitting in the drawing room, addressing letters for Lady Dawley, and the two older women were having tea. The duke's aunt sipped hers and said reflectively to the duchess, "I do believe Edmund is serious about Lady Sophia Heatherstone."

"Do you, Fanny?" replied the duchess. "She is a very lovely girl. Excellent breeding, of course."

"Yes," said Lady Dawley. "She has the dignity and elegance that would be required of the Duchess of Evesham. She would know just how to conduct herself. I think I may say that I have seen all the debutantes these past few years, and he could scarcely do better. Hardy offered for her last year and Sir Robert Bennett, but they say Lady Marley is holding out for a title."

The duchess looked troubled. "I should hate to see Edmund marry a girl who only wanted his title."

"Come, Mama," said Lady Dawley impatiently. "Can you doubt Edmund's ability to attach a woman if only he bothers to exert himself? And I think that this time he may actually *be* exerting himself. He danced with Lady Sophia twice at the Devonshires' ball, and this afternoon he was taking her driving in the park."

Catriona sat as if turned to stone. Both ladies had completely forgotten her presence.

"I understand also that he has given Lettice Moreham her congé." Mrs. Moreham was a very lovely young widow with whom Edmund had enjoyed a discreet affair over the last few years. Catriona had seen her at the theater one night and had noticed the brilliant smile she bestowed on Edmund.

"It is time he settled down," her great-grandmother was saying. "He will be thirty next year."

"I know. I pointed that interesting fact out to him quite recently."

"Oh? And what did he say?"

"Very little. Edmund has always been adept at keeping himself to himself. But he knows his duty. I think he will offer for Lady Sophia."

Catriona made a small, abrupt movement, and both ladies started and stared at her.

"Kate!" said Lady Dawley. "I had quite forgotten you were there."

Catriona swallowed. Her throat felt dry. "I'm finished now," she said a little hoarsely. "May I go upstairs?"

"Of course, child. And thank you," said the duchess kindly.

Catriona walked very steadily to the door and up the stairs to her room. It was not until she reached the safety of this haven that her agitation broke out. She threw herself on her bed and buried her face in her pillow.

"He can't," she whispered fiercely into the soft feathers. "He can't marry her! She's dull and boring and stupid."

But other aspects of Lady Sophia's person and character were eminently desirable. Catriona could not deny that she was very beautiful. And she was well bred—not a bastard. And well-behaved—not a hoyden. She was elegant and would know how to be a duchess. "She'd spoil everything," Catriona said out loud vehemently. "He can't marry her!"

The overheard conversation about Edmund's possible nuptials opened Catriona's eyes to a great number of things she had not previously noticed. She herself was perfectly content as she was; she had always assumed Edmund felt the same.

For the first time she considered her cousin as a man and not simply as her Edmund. Childlike, she had always seen him solely in relation to herself. Now she began to look at him as other people must look.

To other people he was His Grace, the Duke of Burford. The face he showed to her was not the face he showed to society at large. Seen in society, he had an austere elegance and cool manner that was quietly, awesomely, impressive. He was deferred to by all their hostesses, and every dance with him appeared to be regarded by his partner as a personal triumph. "Can you doubt Edmund's ability to attach a woman?" his aunt had asked, and Catriona could not. And aside from his sovereign personal charms, he was one of the richest men in the kingdom. His wife would have one of the best positions in all Britain. These were not considerations that would hold any weight with Catriona, but she had been in London long enough to realize that they weighed very heavily indeed with the world.

*   *   *

The Marquis of Hampton invited Catriona to dance at a particularly crowded ball one evening a few days later, and disregarding the expressed orders of her cousin, she accepted. She remembered the amusing, cynical gossip he had regaled her with on the one other occasion she had danced with him and thought he was the man she needed at the moment.

As they took the floor he murmured to her, "This is a pleasant surprise. You have put me off so many times, Miss MacIan."

"I know." Catriona looked at him candidly. "My cousin says you are a rake."

He gave her a sleepy, seductive smile. He was really quite handsome. "Perhaps I need someone like yourself to reform me," he murmured. Catriona laughed with real amusement. "What is so funny?" he inquired. "Do you think I am such a hardened case?"

"It's not that at all," she replied merrily. "It's just that usually *I'm* the one who needs reforming."

He raised a very defined dark eyebrow. "Really?"

"I'm afraid so," she returned before the movements of the dance swept them apart.

It was a quadrille, and Catriona did not have an opportunity to ask the marquis her question after all. When the dance was over, he put a hand on her elbow. "Why don't you let me

show you the conservatory?" he murmured in
her ear.

"All right," answered Catriona instantly and
let him escort her out of the ballroom and
down the long hall of Chester House.

Chapter Twelve

Neither Catriona nor the marquis had any interest in the conservatory and accorded it a very perfunctory glance.

"I want to know something," Catriona said, turning to him as they stood under a potted palm tree, "and you were the only person I could think of who might tell me."

"Oh?" He gazed down at her in speculation. She was wearing a pale-green dress that caught exactly the shade of her eyes. She looked up at him from under the shelter of half-lowered lashes, a little unsure of his reaction. It was a look of quite unconscious provocation.

"Yes," she said. "Who is Lettice Moreham?"

The marquis's eyes had narrowed as he gazed at Catriona but now they widened again in real surprise. "Lettice Moreham?" he echoed.

"Yes. My aunt said that my cousin Edmund had given her her congé. What does that mean?"

There was a little pause, and then he reached out and captured her hands. "It means, my little siren," he said softly, "that your estimable cousin and the lovely Mrs. Moreham were enjoying an affair and that he has broken it off."

Catriona's lips parted and her eyes widened. "I thought perhaps that was it," she breathed.

The marquis drew her closer to him, and then his hands dropped hers and went to circle her waist. "Now that you have your information, you must pay up," he murmured and bent his head.

Lord Hampton's kiss was very different from Frank's and George's and instinctively Catriona knew that this was the way it should be done. She closed her eyes and put her hands on his shoulders. This was what Edmund did with Lettice Moreham, she thought. Her body was pressed against the marquis's, and under the demanding pressure of his mouth her lips parted. Did Edmund do *this*? she thought with a little thrill of shocked surprise. Her head was pressed back against the marquis's arm, and his other hand came up and lightly cupped her breast. Catriona jumped like a scalded cat and pulled away from him.

"That's more than kissing!" she accused from a safer distance.

His eyes were slits, and he was breathing

hard. He reached for her again. "God," he said. "I wish you'd let me teach you . . ."

"No, thank you," she said decidedly. She had moved quite out of his reach now. "I shouldn't have kissed you, either, but it seemed only fair. I think we had better go back. Lady Dawley will be looking for me."

"Catriona," came Edmund's voice from the doorway. "Come here." She knew that tone and moved instantly to obey him. "Go to your aunt," he said when she reached his side. She cast a brief glance at his face, said nothing, but lifted her skirt and ran.

She was sitting demurely with Lady Dawley when the duke came back into the ballroom. Edmund did not come over to her, nor did he speak to her during the rest of the evening. When they arrived home, he said, "I want to see you, Catriona, before you go to bed."

Margaret, to whom Catriona had hastily confided her escapade, gave her a look of mixed terror and sympathy before she fled upstairs, followed more slowly by Lady Dawley. Catriona trailed after Edmund to the library. He did not ask her to sit but demanded, almost as soon as the door was closed behind him, "Did you deliberately disobey me and go off to the conservatory with Hampton?"

Catriona bit her lip. "Yes, Edmund."

"God damn it," he almost shouted, "don't you know what kind of man he is? It isn't safe for a young girl to be alone with a man of his stamp."

He was really very angry; he rarely swore.

"But Edmund," she said in a small voice, "what could he possibly do to me? We were in the conservatory!"

He stared at her, his gray eyes unreadable. "Did he kiss you?" he asked.

Catriona hesitated. She could lie successfully to most of the people she knew, but not, unfortunately, to Edmund. She looked at the carpet. "Yes," she whispered.

He moved, and when she looked up it was to find him sitting in a chair, staring into the dying fire. His usual look of impeccable worldly elegance was quite gone. His black hair was faintly disheveled, his immaculately tied cravat loosened as if he had tugged at it. She stared for a minute at his profile. She knew the look of him so well, the set of his shoulders and collarbone, the sweep of lashes against the hard line of his cheek, the beautiful, sensitive hands, the shape of his fingernails. . . . Had he touched Lettice Moreham's breast as Lord Hampton had touched hers?

She felt her stomach suddenly clench. She balled her hands into fists to keep from reaching out toward him. His face blurred before her eyes. He looked up and misread the expression on her face.

"Don't look so frightened, Catriona," he said wearily. Then, with an attempt at humor, "I'm not going to beat you."

Her heart was hammering so hard that she was certain he must hear it. "I—" she began and then stopped. She had no idea of what to say.

"I know Hampton is attractive to women," he was going on carefully, "but he will only hurt you, Catriona. He is not the marrying kind."

"I—I only wanted to ask him a question," she said a little wildly. "I don't think he's attractive at all."

"Oh?" She had not sat down, and now he rose and faced her. "What question?"

She stared straight ahead into his cravat. The top of her head barely reached his shoulder, and she knew a wild desire to throw herself at him, to beg him to hold and comfort her as he had in the past. For a brief second she wanted desperately for him to be to her as he always had.

"Catriona?" he said, and she looked up and saw the beautiful, chiseled line of his mouth.

The old Catriona would have told him what her question had been but the new, awakened Catriona merely shook her head. He repeated her name, his voice becoming edged with impatience. Then the door opened.

"For goodness sake, Edmund," said the duchess, "let this child go to bed. It's too late and too cold to be keeping her up. You can scold her in the morning."

There was a pause, and then Edmund said, "That won't be necessary, Grandmama. I have said all I mean to say on the subject. Good night, Catriona."

"Good night, Edmund," she got out. "I'm sorry." She left the room under the protection of her great-grandmother.

But once she got to her own room there was no protection from her thoughts. Something had happened to her in the library that she could not ignore. For the first time her feelings for Edmund had clarified themselves, and she understood what they were.

He had always been the center of her emotional life. All her accomplishments had been achieved in an effort to please him. A month in London had been enough to show her that she was far better educated than other young girls of her age, far better read. She had no illusions about her own genius. It was because of Edmund that she understood Burke's political theory and could talk to Lord Morton, that she understood Descartes' reasoning and could so astonish Mr. Hardy. It was because of Edmund that she knew of the great achievements of Newton and Herschel. It was because of Edmund that she spoke fluent French and played the piano well. Throughout all the years of her education his had been the intelligence that prodded her, the wit that delighted her, the approval that rewarded her for her efforts.

She had always known she loved him. Now for the first time she understood the nature of that love. And she understood also that it was not a love that could be reciprocated. In his eyes she was a little sister to whom he would always offer his protection and his affection.

That other aspect of love, the one she had discovered as she stared tonight at the line of his cheek, his mouth, his hands, did not enter into his feelings for her.

She was his little cousin, Diccon's daughter. And even if by some wild chance of fate he had come to look at her as a woman, there could be no future for them together. She was not good enough for him. She was a bastard. And he, she knew with all the instincts of her deeply passionate heart, he was the only man she would ever love.

It was a very long night for Catriona, the most painful night of her entire young life. By the time the first light of dawn came seeping into her room she had come to the bitter conclusion that she must marry. Edmund expected her to marry; that was why he had brought her to London at such cost. She was not there, as she had previously thought, solely to be a companion to Margaret. She was there to find a husband and settle her future for good. She could not spend the rest of her life at Evesham Castle.

Catriona did not cry. The pain was too great for tears to be a relief. Her duty as she saw it now was to make things easy for Edmund. He must never suspect how she felt about him. She would be pleasant and obedient and marry whomever he chose. It was the only honorable path open to her.

Chapter Thirteen

If popularity on the dance floor was anything
to judge by, Catriona was having a very successful season. The real test of success, however,
was a marriage offer, and so far there had
been none forthcoming. The Earl of Wareham
was certainly taken by Catriona, but, as Lady
Dawley confided to her mother, there was little hope of his ever coming up to scratch.

"Eugenia Wareham won't allow it," said Lady
Dawley definitely. "Let's be frank, Mama. If
the people involved are high-born enough, illegitimacy may be overlooked. But that is not
the case with Kate. Diccon was the cousin of a
duke, but he himself was only a plain gentleman with a comfortable property and income.
And who was Kate's mother? A Highland girl.
No, Mama. We can have no hope of Wareham."

"Perhaps the young man will have a different idea," replied the duchess. "In my experience young men do not always follow their mother's wishes."

"In this case he will," said Lady Dawley. "Wareham is a very amiable young man, but he thinks a great deal of his position. Don't try to persuade yourself that he doesn't."

The duchess sighed. "What about Mr. Hardy?"

"He is a possibility," Lady Dawley acknowledged. "His family is good, but not noble. And he has plenty of money. He may think a connection with Burford would outweigh all the disadvantages of such a union."

The duchess stared at her daughter for perhaps ten seconds, then said flatly, "I would rather see Kate married to Frank Winthrop. Or to her cousin George, for that matter. I was not in favor of bringing her to London and I am beginning to think it was a very great mistake."

Lady Dawley frowned. "What do you mean, Mama? She has taken far better than I ever dreamed possible."

The duchess rose. "I mean that Kate has the most loving heart in the world, and it distresses me unutterably to hear her discussed as if she were a piece of goods put up to market."

"Come, Mama," said Lady Dawley impatiently. "I don't say that affection is not an important part of marriage. But considerations of station, fortune, and property are important as well."

"Edmund should not have brought Kate to London," repeated the duchess before she turned to go upstairs to her room.

Catriona had come to the same conclusion as her grandmother. For the first time since she had made her appearance in society she was aware of the insecurity of her own status. She had known before of course that she was unacceptable to some people, but it had not mattered to her. In fact, it had been a protection. She didn't want anyone to marry her. She had been shielded by her false assumption that when the season was over, she and Edmund would go back to Evesham and resume their old life. It was not overhearing herself called a bastard that had so upset her at her first Almack's assembly; it had been the sight of Edmund dancing with the beautiful Lady Sophia Heatherstone.

But now it seemed that she would have to marry. She thought about all the men she had met in London and came to the conclusion that the one she liked best was the Marquis of Hampton. Edmund, unfortunately, didn't like him, and she had thought to marry whomever Edmund chose for her. However, as the days went by, the round of parties and balls and drives in the park that she had originally found so entertaining began to lose its flavor for her. The young men who danced with her and drove her in the park were very pleasant, but she found them all a trifle dull. The marquis, she thought, would not be dull at least. And being so disreputable himself, he might not mind her own status. Edmund had said he was not the marrying kind, but perhaps, Catriona thought a little daringly, perhaps she might make him change his mind.

She saw him for the first time after the Chesters' ball at the theater. She was sitting in a box with Edmund, Lady Dawley, the duchess, Margaret, Margaret's Mr. Halley, and her own escort, Mr. Hardy, waiting for the curtain to go up. Catriona listened to Lady Dawley's light chatter with only half an ear, conscious only of the blissful torture of Edmund's presence close behind her. She didn't have to turn around to know where he was. She could feel him in every nerve of her body. She knew now why she had always been so acutely conscious of his presence, why in the largest of crowds she had always known unerringly where he was. He said something to Mr. Hardy in a low voice, and Catriona bit her lip. She gazed around the theater desperately, trying to beat down her feelings, and caught the eye of Lord Hampton in the opposite box. He raised a hand to her, and Catriona, with her back safely to Edmund, smiled at him.

During the intermission she went for a stroll with Mr. Hardy, Meg, and Mr. Halley, and they met, quite by chance, the Marquis of Hampton. They all stood chatting for a minute, and then the marquis said to Catriona in a low voice, "I am afraid I have been warned off,

Miss MacIan, otherwise I would have called on you."

Catriona looked sympathetic. "Edmund can be very intimidating," she agreed softly.

The marquis's sleepy eyes glinted. They were really a very nice shade of blue, she thought. "*I* am not intimidated," he murmured. "I thought that perhaps you were."

Catriona gave him a long green look. "We are going to Vauxhall tomorrow night," she said, seemingly at random. "I hear it is supposed to be very enjoyable."

The marquis's blue eyes now looked amused. "It is," he said. "I enjoy it myself."

"Do you?" she asked innocently and turned as she felt Meg's hand on her arm.

"The next act is beginning, Kate," said Margaret's soft voice.

Catriona smiled at the marquis. "Good evening, Lord Hampton," she said sweetly. "It was very pleasant talking to you."

"Good evening, Miss MacIan," he replied gravely.

They went to Vauxhall the following evening: Margaret, Mr. Halley, Lady Dawley, Catriona, and Lord Wareham. Lady Dawley had been surprised and triumphant when Wareham had asked to accompany them. She had accepted his escort graciously. Edmund was away for a few days, visiting William Herschel at Slough, and Lord Wareham was a distinct addition to their party.

Catriona wore a dress of palest pink, a color
that flattered her complexion and was thought
suitable for young girls in their first season.
But there was nothing childlike about Catriona's
face, and Lady Dawley, catching sight of Lord
Wareham's eyes as he looked at her charge's
profile, was startled. Perhaps, she thought, as
her own eyes rested on Catriona's averted face,
perhaps she had underestimated Kate's attrac-
tion.

Vauxhall Pleasure Gardens consisted of a
series of walks and alleys lit by a quantity of
lanterns and lamps. In the center of the gardens was a large open space with a rotunda for
dancing and tiers of boxes where refreshments
were served.

Catriona was delighted with the glowing gardens and the box where they sat. Several people they knew came over to greet them and
shake hands. As the orchestra started up again,
Lord Wareham turned to Catriona and asked
if she would care to dance. She accepted, and
the two of them moved off toward the Rotunda.

Halfway through the evening Lord Wareham's sister, Lady Elizabeth Atwood, made an
appearance at their box and, after frigidly greet-
ing Lady Dawley and the rest of the party,
virtually demanded that her brother dance with
her. Lord Wareham looked very annoyed, but
his manners were too good to permit him to do
anything but excuse himself and accompany
his sister to the Rotunda.

Two minutes later Lord Hampton appeared

and asked Catriona to dance. "I'd love to," Catriona replied instantly, before her chaperone could object. Lady Dawley frowned but made no move to stop Catriona from leaving the box with the marquis.

"Instead of dancing, why don't we take a stroll through the gardens?" he asked as they neared the Rotunda.

"I should like to see the gardens," Catriona said. "They look so beautiful in all this lovely golden lamplight."

Lord Hampton drew her hand through his arm, and they began to stroll down a path. "The gardens are not the only thing that looks lovely in the lamplight," he remarked, looking down at her.

"If you mean me, thank you," she returned easily.

He smiled. "For—how old—eighteen?—you have become very adept at dealing with compliments."

"Seventeen." She looked up at him a little gravely. "I find people in London give a great many compliments. It is a little difficult to pay much heed to them."

"I see. You would prize them more if they came more rarely. I must remember not to compliment you again."

Catriona laughed. "Oh, dear. Now I have done myself in."

There was a pause as they passed another couple returning toward the Rotunda. Then Lord Hampton said, "Your cousin the duke would not like it if he knew you were walking here with me."

"You do not need to tell me that," replied Catriona vigorously. She looked up at him curiously. "How does one get to be a rake? Does it mean you have had a great many mistresses?"

He laughed. "You are very astute for one so young, Miss MacIan."

"But a great many men who are not rakes also have mistresses," she went on. "What is the difference? Does it have to do with the numbers?"

His shoulders were shaking a little. "Numbers have something to do with it," he agreed.

"Hmm," said Catriona and walked beside him in silence for a minute. "How many mistresses have you had?" she asked finally.

"Dozens," he replied gravely.

"Dozens. Goodness." She looked up at him and then smiled impishly. "How exhausting."

He didn't say anything for a minute and then asked, "May I ask why this detailed inquiry into my love life?"

"Well, I don't know anything at all about rakes and mistresses, you see, and I wanted to find out. I'm afraid that when I'm interested in something I ask a great many questions. But as Edmund always told me, questions are the way to knowledge."

"Yes, well, I rather doubt this is the sort of knowledge he was talking about."

Catriona giggled. "So do I, actually."

"Kate." The marquis stopped walking and turned her to face him. "Why did you invite me to Vauxhall tonight?"

Catriona didn't quibble. "Because I like you," she replied simply. "You don't act as if I were a stupid, mindless, hysterical idiot." Her eyes danced. "If I had asked those questions of Lord Wareham," she said, "he would have fainted."

He imagined the scene and grinned. "He would have," he agreed.

"And I don't see how your being a rake has anything to do with me," she went on. "All those ladies became your mistress of their own free will, I presume. You didn't force them."

She looked at him inquiringly, and his shoulders shook again. "No," he got out. "I don't go in for rape."

"I didn't think so," she said seriously. "And I have no intention of becoming your mistress. It would break my great-grandmother's heart should I ever do such a thing. So it seems to me all the danger Edmund talks about is entirely in his own imagination."

"The danger may be to your reputation, not your morals," he said and now he was serious.

Catriona's face became suddenly very still. "That's true," she said. "I hadn't thought of that. People might say, 'Like mother like daughter.'"

She had thought her voice was expressionless, but something of her feeling must have shown, for he said roughly, "What swine said that to you?"

She bent her head. "What does it matter? It's true, isn't it?"

"No, it is not. Or if it is, it will only be said because people are jealous."

"Jealous." She looked up at him out of wide eyes. "Edmund said that too. But why should anyone be jealous of me?"

"Because, Kate," he murmured, bending toward her upturned face, "there isn't a man in London who isn't longing to do this." Catriona closed her eyes and then, as the pressure of his mouth increased, raised her arms and slid them around his neck. Really, she thought, feeling his body pressed to hers, this was very pleasant. She could quite see why he had so many mistresses.

Chapter Fourteen

On their way back to Lady Dawley, Catriona and Lord Hampton met Louisa Worthing, who was walking with her brother, Frederick, a man Catriona did not know, and Sarah Worthing, Louisa's sister. During the course of the season Louisa had not proved to be one of Catriona's admirers. She had several times made spiteful remarks about Catriona's dress or behavior within her hearing. And it had been Lady Maria Worthing, Louisa's mother, who had uttered the malicious comment about Catriona the night of her first Almack's assembly.

Louisa's whole face sharpened to alertness now as she saw Catriona walking alone with the Marquis of Hampton. "Miss MacIan," she said frostily, her dark eyes going from Catriona to the marquis.

Catriona smiled sunnily. "How are you, Miss Worthing?" She included the whole party in her smile. "Such a lovely evening for a stroll. Lord Hampton and I have been quite enchanted by the beauty of the gardens."

"Indeed," said Louisa and glared at her brother, who was beaming fatuously at Catriona.

"Indeed," said the marquis. "Good evening." He took Catriona's arm and steered her firmly past the two couples and along the path toward the pavilion.

"Oh, dear," said Catriona. "Now I am in the suds. Louisa will have the news of our stroll all over London tomorrow."

"What a repellent girl she is," he remarked distastefully.

"I feel sorry for her," said Catriona. "She must be terribly unhappy."

"What makes you say that?" he asked in surprise.

"Happy people don't feel the need to spread unhappiness," Catriona replied simply.

The marquis stopped for a moment and looked down at her. His smile was a little twisted. "That is a very profound statement," he said.

She laughed. "Not at all. It's only common sense, my lord."

He began to walk on. "It is only common sense for you not to see me again, Kate. Do you know that?"

She sighed. "Yes, I suppose that is true. Edmund will be furious when he hears I've been walking with you." She lowered her voice and said on a note of horror, *"Alone."*

He grinned. "I want to see you again. Very much."

"I'd like to see you too," she replied frankly. "But I really don't see how."

"I'll come up with a scheme," he promised as they reached the end of the path and came into the lighted area where the boots were. "I've had a lot of experience," he added, and Catriona chuckled. Lady Dawley was awaiting them, and the marquis handed Catriona over and made a graceful exit.

The story of Catriona's clandestine walk with Lord Hampton was not in fact spread all over London the next day. The ton was regaled with quite another scandal. Lady Louisa Worthing had eloped with the younger son of the village parson—in fact, the very young man whom Catriona had seen her with at Vauxhall the previous evening. Lord Worthing had gone after them, but nothing had been heard from him as yet.

The news got out by way of the servants, and half of London was agog. "But what is so terrible?" Catriona asked her great-grandmother. "They were heading for Scotland, so they are planning to marry."

"It is a very unequal match, my dear, which is why the Worthings won't allow it," the duchess responded gently. "Louisa will have rather a lot of money, and this boy is practically penniless. The Worthings are a very old family, and the boy, though a gentleman, can hardly be called well born. It seems the two of them grew up together. It is a thousand pities that this has happened. Either way, Louisa will be ruined."

"But why will she be ruined, Grandmama?"

"She won't be received in society, my dear. If Lord Worthing catches them and stops the marriage, she will still have been alone in the young man's company overnight. And if they do reach Scotland, the likelihood is that her family will refuse to recognize her again."

Catriona's eyes flashed. "How utterly unfair."

"Perhaps it is," said the duchess, "but it is the way of the world, my dear."

Rumors abounded, and the following day the news got out that Lord Worthing had recovered his daughter. The young couple had not managed to reach Scotland after all. The boy had been sent packing back to the country and Louisa had been brought back to London.

Three days later Catriona attended a rout at the home of Mrs. Mason-Burgley. It was not a large affair, but many of the ton's most important figures were present. Edmund had returned from Slough in the late afternoon and accompanied his aunt and his two wards. Catriona was surprised to see that Lord Hampton was also present. This was not the kind of party he usually attended.

There was a great deal of mingling and chat-

ting among the guests. There was to be dancing in one of the rooms and cards in another,
but neither activity had gotten underway.
Catriona was standing with Lady Dawley and
Lord Wareham when a sudden hush came over
the room. She looked up, and there on the
threshold was Lady Worthing. Next to her,
pale and frightened-looking, stood Louisa. There
was a dreadful moment of silence, and then
the lady standing closest to Louisa started to
turn her back.

Suddenly the silence was broken by a warm,
friendly voice. "Louisa!" said Catriona as she
moved swiftly across the floor. "How lovely to
see you."

Louisa turned apprehensive eyes on Catriona's face. "Th-thank you," she almost whispered.

There was a little movement behind Catriona.
"I've managed to secure a few chairs, Catriona,"
said Edmund's voice close to her ear. "Why
don't you and Miss Worthing come along and
sit down and I'll get you some refreshment."

Catriona's green eyes were blazing. "Thank
you, Edmund," she said. As Edmund took
Louisa's arm, it was as if a spell had been
broken, and the room relaxed into chatter.
The three of them crossed the room, and as
they passed Lady Dawley and Lord Wareham,
Catriona stopped. "Do you care to join us, my
lord?" she asked.

Lord Wareham wanted no part of this awk-
ward situation. He opened his mouth to de-

cline and found himself caught in the green blaze of Catriona's stare. He realized with unusual perception that if he refused to accompany her now, he would have lost her for good. He swallowed. "I'd be delighted to, Miss MacIan," he said, and Catriona rewarded him with a dazzling smile.

So it was that Louisa Worthing, instead of finding herself a social outcast, sat and danced and had supper with the two highest-born and most eligible bachelors in London.

"I would have helped you out," Lord Hampton said to Catriona as they danced together later, "but I thought you needed someone of more notable rectitude than I."

Catriona laughed. "Poor Lord Wareham. He wanted no part of Louisa. Or me. But he served his purpose." She glanced over her shoulder to where Louisa was dancing with Mr. Hardy. All of Catriona's admirers had quickly realized where their duty lay.

"If he didn't want any part of you, he wouldn't have done it," said the marquis, and Catriona shrugged a little in acknowledgment. "Your cousin didn't need any prompting, though," Lord Hampton continued.

"No." Catriona's lovely, full mouth was a little compressed.

There was always a sense of strain whenever he mentioned her cousin. The marquis could not tell what her feelings toward him really were. "It was not the sort of thing I would have expected him to do," he said probingly. "He always looks so cool and unconcerned."

"He's not like that at all," said Catriona. "It's just that most people don't know him very well."

"He's not precisely an easy chap to get to know," the marquis responded ruefully.

"I suppose that's true," said Catriona. "But he was as angry as I was about what they were all doing to Louisa."

"That girl has done nothing but malign you since you came to London," Lord Hampton said slowly. "You know that."

"Yes. I told you she was unhappy. All the time she has wanted to marry this boy, and her parents wouldn't let her. Poor thing."

"Do you know what you have, Kate?" He was speaking slowly, as though discovering something. "A kind heart."

Catriona shrugged again. "That's not so unusual."

He laughed a little, and for a minute his hand on hers tightened possessively. "Oh, yes, it is," he contradicted her positively. "Kindness and compassion are two qualities sadly missing from the makeup of most of the people I know."

They were not missing from Edmund's character, Catriona thought as she made some response to the marquis. Over his shoulder she caught sight of the duke's black head. He was listening courteously to Mrs. Mason-Burgley and had reverted to his usual air of cool, worldly elegance.

They none of them really knew Edmund, she thought to herself as her eyes stayed fastened on his beautiful, chiseled face. He had grace and compassion, wisdom and integrity. Everything she knew about justice and responsibility she had learned from him. And he had too the gift of laughter. She remembered, with suddenly vivid immediacy, the crazy rhymes he used to make up for her, the funny songs and outrageous riddles. It was probably a side of him only she had seen. "I beg your pardon?" she said to Lord Hampton. The marquis repeated his comment, and after a second she made a suitable reply.

Chapter Fifteen

It was not until the evening was almost over that Catriona danced with Edmund. It was a waltz, and as his arms went around her, she felt her breath catch and she stiffened. But his guiding arms were competent and impersonal, and after a minute she began to relax. When the dance was over, he kept her hand in his and began to walk toward the open French windows. Catriona accompanied him in silence, and soon the two of them were standing side by side looking out at the small garden of Mrs. Mason-Burgley's town house.

"I was very proud of you tonight, Catriona," Edmund said softly. "Louisa Worthing may be a wretched girl, but she doesn't deserve to be publicly humiliated."

"It was rotten, Edmund," Catriona said

warmly. "All those people were going to ignore her."

"Yes. They were." He raised an eyebrow. "Charming, isn't it?"

"It's so hypocritical!" she cried. "Half the women in that room have lovers, but they were going to turn their backs on Louisa because she spent one night alone with a boy she loved. A boy she was trying to marry!" Catriona turned to him, her eyes flashing.

He smiled at her, his rare, warm smile that she had seen so often as a child and saw so seldom now. "The only times you ever get angry," he said, "are when you're angry on someone else's behalf."

She smiled back. "I think I frightened poor Lord Wareham half to death."

Edmund began to laugh. "Did you see his face as we were sitting there?"

Catriona giggled. "He looked like a stuffed fish."

"A flounder, I thought," Edmund got out, and then they both were sobbing with laughter, hanging onto the balcony railings to keep standing up. "Oh, God," said Edmund, trying to sober up.

"L-louisa looked l-like . . ." Catriona began, and Edmund finished for her. "A l-lemon sole." And they were both off again.

There was a step behind them, and both turned to see Lord Wareham standing there. "I beg your pardon, Your Grace," he said stiffly to the still hysterical Edmund. "I was looking for Miss MacIan. I have this dance."

"H-here she is," said Edmund unsteadily.

"Not flounder," said Catriona suddenly. "Trout." And the two of them were shaken by another gale of hilarity.

Finally Lord Wareham's silent outrage registered on Edmund. "I do beg your pardon, Wareham," he managed. "Go along and have your dance, Catriona."

"Yes," said Catriona. She wiped her eyes with her handkerchief. "Sorry, my lord." She moved toward him, and as she did so the music stopped. "Oh, dear, I'm afraid the dance is over. I'm so sorry." She cast a brief look at his stiff face and choked. Behind her she could hear Edmund ostentatiously begin to cough. Her lips trembled.

"There you are, Miss MacIan," came the voice of the Marquis of Hampton. "I believe this is my dance."

Catriona could feel the change in Edmund. Without looking at him, she said, "Yes, it is," put her hand on the marquis's arm, and made a hasty exit toward the dance floor.

The dance with Lord Hampton was the last one of the evening, and as he stood on the pavement in front of Mrs. Mason-Burgley's house, the marquis was joined by Lord Wareham. This in itself was an unusual circumstance, and the marquis glanced at him in great surprise as the young earl fell into step with him.

"An extraordinary evening," said Lord Wareham stiffly. "Miss MacIan's actions do credit to her warm heart, of course, but one could hope that her guardian would guide her along a wiser course."

"Burford, do you mean?" asked the marquis.

"Yes. Of course, he has always been a little odd himself. He may understand the intricacies of the solar system, but he is not so well versed in the intricacies of social niceties. Still, I would have thought even he would have the sense to stop his cousin from actions that could very easily damage her own standing."

"Far from curbing her, I should say rather he aided and abetted her," remarked the marquis.

"He certainly did!" Lord Wareham's full indignation broke loose. "Then he took her out on the balcony during *my* dance, and when I went to claim her they were both out there laughing like—like lunatics."

"Burford?" said the marquis.

"He was hanging onto the railing," said Lord Wareham disapprovingly. "Extremely undignified."

"And unexpected," murmured Lord Hampton. "I begin to think Miss MacIan was right when she said that most people did not know the duke. He appears to have unexpected depths."

"He was damn rude." Lord Wareham was now looking sulky. "So was Miss MacIan. And that isn't like her at all. She is usually—angelic."

The marquis's blue eyes began to glint in the way that Catriona admired. "I don't think I should call her an angel, Wareham," he said. "Hell-raiser might be a better term."

Lord Wareham made an indignant sound and stalked off into the night.

All the way home in the coach Catriona was forced to listen to Lady Dawley expatiating on her rash behavior. Her ladyship got no encouragement from her companions, however, for Edmund merely repeated that he was proud of Catriona and Margaret called her brave and generous.

"Brave and generous, perhaps," said Lady Dawley, "but hardly wise."

"Well, I hope I'm never wise if it means I must act like a hypocrite and a fraud," Catriona said vigorously.

"Speaking of wisdom," said Edmund, and the three women stiffened at the note in his voice, "I thought I told you it was not wise to encourage Hampton. You danced with him twice tonight."

For the second time that night Catriona lost her temper. It was outrageous of Edmund, she thought, to insist on marrying her off and not even to let her make her own choice. And he was not being fair to the marquis, which—though she didn't think of this at the moment—was quite unlike him.

"I fail to see why Lord Hampton should be such a pariah, Edmund," she said hotly. "He is in the same situation as Louisa. I daresay there isn't a man in London who doesn't keep a mistress"—she glared at his shadowy figure seated across from her in the darkness of the coach—"present company included." There was a stifled sound from Margaret, but Catriona swept on unheeding, "Yet you are all ready to act as if he were the only man in the world who went around seducing females. At least he's honest! He doesn't pretend to be what he's not. And he's not trying to seduce me. He's my friend. He likes me. And I like him. I like him a great deal better than all the stuffed fish that *you* approve of. He's—he's real. He's one of the few real people I've met in London."

There was a moment of frozen silence. Then Edmund said frigidly, "Have you quite finished?"

She sat back against the squabs. Her heart was hammering. She thought everyone in the coach must hear it. "Yes, I have."

"Good," said Edmund, "because I think we have all of us had quite enough of your puerile philosophy." The coach came to a halt in front of Burford House, and Edmund opened the door before the footman could get to it and jumped out. "I'm going for a walk," he said savagely and stalked off into the darkness.

Both Lady Dawley and Meg regarded Catriona with a mixture of awe and fear. "You shouldn't have spoken to Edmund like that, Kate," murmured Lady Dawley at last.

"I'm glad I did," Catriona returned, unrepentent. "Everything I said was perfectly true. Edmund is nothing but a—a whited sepulcher!"

Her defiance did not last for very long, however, and once she got into bed, the tears began to slide down her cheeks. She felt very alone and very miserable. She cried herself to sleep.

Chapter Sixteen

The following day the Marquis of Hampton received a note from the Duke of Burford asking him to call at Burford House later in the morning. The marquis complied with the request and presented himself in Grosvenor Square at precisely eleven-thirty. He was shown into the library, where the duke awaited him.

"Please be seated, Hampton," said Edmund civilly and watched the other man in silence as he settled himself in a leather armchair. There was no denying that the marquis was a good-looking specimen. His thick, curly brown hair was well cut. He had good features and very blue eyes. He was as tall as Edmund.

"I want to talk to you about my cousin Catriona," the duke said without further preamble. "I am concerned about the attention you are paying to her."

"I am paying her no more attention than half a dozen other men," the marquis pointed out reasonably.

"Those half-dozen men who do not have your reputation."

The marquis looked sardonic. "No. They are more discreet."

Edmund leaned back in his chair. "That is what Catriona said."

The marquis's surprise was genuine. "She did?"

"Yes. In fact she compared your case to Louisa Worthing's."

A look of disgust crossed the marquis's handsome face, and Edmund laughed. "I perfectly appreciate your feelings, Hampton. Louisa Worthing is a most unworthy female."

"She has been saying the most malicious things about your cousin ever since she came to town. Do you know that?"

"Yes. And so does Catriona." Edmund looked gravely at the man seated across the desk from him. "But Catriona does not have a mean bone in her body. She has some failings, but unkindness is not one of them."

The marquis returned Edmund's look measuringly. "And what *are* her faults then, Your Grace?"

"She does not foresee consequences." Edmund's gaze did not falter. "And she is not properly aware of her own power of provocation. She follows the impulse of her own warm heart and doesn't understand where that may lead her. I am very concerned, Hampton, about your setting her up as your latest flirt. It won't do her reputation any good, but that is not so important as the likelihood that she is going to get hurt. And I am telling you now that I will not allow that to happen."

"She is not my latest flirt," said the marquis slowly. "I don't flirt with seventeen-year-olds."

"Then may I ask what you *are* doing?" said Edmund in a voice the marquis had never heard before.

His head jerked up a little, and he stared into the duke's dark eyes. There was a controlled force about the man that was distinctly unnerving. "Actually," said the marquis, and his own voice sounded strange now, "I want to marry her."

There was a flicker of some emotion in the dark-gray eyes, and then a shutter seemed to come down. "So," said Edmund softly. "And Catriona?"

"I don't know. I think she likes me but I haven't mentioned marriage."

"She does like you." Edmund's face was expressionless. "She told me so last night."

"Did she?" The marquis raised an eyebrow. "Were you telling her to stay away from me?"

"Yes. If you were in my position, Hampton, you would have done the same."

The marquis smiled a little crookedly. "I suppose I should. But the situation has changed, I believe."

"Yes. So it seems." Edmund regarded him

for a long minute in silence, and finally the marquis got to his feet.

"Look, Burford, I perfectly understand all the objections that are going through your mind. A man with my past, my reputation, has no business wanting to marry a girl just out of the schoolroom. I know that, and dammit it's true. But Kate is no ordinary schoolroom miss, and you know it." He turned around and faced Edmund. "She wouldn't be happy with a boy, Burford. Or with a cold fish like Wareham. I think she would be happy with me." He took a few steps closer to the desk. "When first I met her I saw what every other man in town saw. But there is far more to Kate than just that extraordinary magnetism. There isn't another woman in the world who would have done what she did last night for Louisa Worthing."

"No," said Edmund. "There isn't."

"I am a rich man, Burford. And the title is good value even if its owner is a bit tarnished. I don't care about her parents or about her dowry. All I want is Kate."

For the first time in the interview Edmund was not looking at the marquis. He laid his flawless hands on the desk top and regarded them intently. "I think perhaps you are right, that you could make Catriona happy."

"I love her, you see," said the marquis quietly.

Edmund looked preoccupied. "Yes, I do see." He stood up. "Well, that will be all then, Hampton. I presume you would prefer to speak to Catriona yourself."

"Yes, I should."

"She is not at home now, but you may call back at two this afternoon. You'll find her in."

Edmund began to move some papers on his desk, as if he were anxious to get back to work. The marquis glanced at the neat pile of mathematical calculations. "Well, I won't keep you any longer, Burford. We'll speak again after I get Kate's consent."

The beautiful, long-fingered hands stilled on the paper. "You seem very certain of her," said Edmund.

"Do I?" The marquis's eyes were on Edmund's hands. "Well, I'm not. In some ways, and contrary to appearances, Kate is not at all easy to know. I have no idea really what she'll say." He nodded abruptly. "Good day, Burford."

"Good day." Edmund's eyes were inscrutable as he watched the door close behind the marquis's broad-shouldered back. Then he picked up the paper he had ostentatiously been working on and tore it, again and again, with a violence that was all the more frightening because it was so controlled.

Catriona had gone with Margaret and Lady Dawley to Hookham's library. When they returned to Grosvenor Square, there was a phaeton being walked up and down in front of the house. Margaret grew very flushed, and Catriona and Lady Dawley glanced at her inquiringly.

"Do you know who that phaeton belongs to, Meg?" asked her ladyship.

"I believe—that is, it might be Mr. Halley's," said Margaret a little breathlessly. "He said he was going to call on Edmund this morning."

Catriona smiled. "Meg, how wonderful." She squeezed her cousin's arm with warm affection.

"Do you think Edmund will approve of him?" Margaret asked Lady Dawley anxiously.

"Certainly. He is an unexceptional young man," said Lady Dawley, who had already checked him out thoroughly.

As they moved toward the staircase, the library door opened, and Edmund appeared on the threshold. "Meg," he said gently, "would you come into the library for a few minutes, please?"

"Yes, of course, Edmund." Margaret threw a brief look at Catriona and got an encouraging smile in return. Then she disappeared into the library, and Edmund closed the door. He had not looked at Catriona.

Forty-five minutes later Margaret knocked on Catriona's door. Her cheeks were flushed a pale rose, and she looked extremely pretty. "I'm engaged," she said to Catriona and smiled radiantly.

"Meg, I'm so happy for you." Catriona embraced her tall cousin warmly. "How lucky you are to be marrying the man you love." She hoped her envy did not show in her voice.

"Yes, I know." Margaret laughed. "What would I have done if Edmund had refused?"

"Eloped, of course," said Catriona practically. "And successfully, not like Louisa Worthing. How stupid she was to get caught."

Margaret was gazing at Catriona in horror. "You don't mean that, Kate."

Catriona looked surprised. "Of course I mean it. If I were going to elope with the man I loved, I should take very good care no one could find me. Louisa stupidly stayed on the main road."

"But Kate, it would take days to get to Scotland by any other route."

"So?"

Margaret suddenly laughed. "How like you, Kate. You wouldn't care, would you?"

"Of course not. I'd take care to get myself good and compromised. Then they would have to let me marry."

"It will be much easier if Edmund approves your choice," advised Margaret, still laughing.

Catriona turned to look out the window. "Yes," she said over her shoulder. "It would, wouldn't it?"

Chapter Seventeen

Catriona was curled up on the window seat in her bedroom, reading the book she had borrowed from Hookham's library that morning, when one of the housemaids appeared to inform her the duke wished to see her in the morning room. Catriona's mouth went dry. He was going to speak to her about her outburst last night. She had a sudden cowardly impulse to say she was sick and couldn't come. She didn't want to fight with Edmund any more. But instead she rose and went to inspect herself in the mirror before she went downstairs.

Her hair was smooth and shining, her apricot walking dress relatively unwrinkled. She straightened her shoulders and walked out the door and down the stairs. All of the fiery defiance of last night was gone. She would apologize, she thought. She had said terrible things to him. She could not bear Edmund to be angry with her.

She pushed open the morning room door a little.

"Come in, Catriona," said Edmund.

Catriona stepped into the room, and her eyes widened as she saw the Marquis of Hampton. "My—my lord," she said uncertainly.

"Lord Hampton has something he wishes to say to you, Catriona." Edmund's voice seemed to be coming from very far away. "I'll be in the library," he said to the marquis, and then he was gone, closing the door and leaving her alone with the marquis.

There was a moment of silence, and then Lord Hampton said, "Don't look so startled, Kate. I have something to ask you, and your cousin has given me permission to see you alone."

Catriona stared at him blankly. "Last night he was angry because I danced with you twice."

"Yes, I know." The marquis crossed the room and took her hands in his. "Kate," he said softly, "I know I have led a very wicked life. All those mistresses and so forth."

Catriona's eyes gleamed. "Dozens," she said.

"Yes, well, I've called a halt to all that. That is, I will call a halt to it." He drew her closer to him. "If only you will promise to marry me," he finished.

Catriona's head was tipped far back to look into his face. He was deadly serious, she recognized that. She was suddenly a little frightened that she had brought him to this point so quickly. She had scarcely crooked her finger. She bit her lip. "Are you quite certain you want to marry me, my lord?"

His firm, well-cut mouth curved slightly. "I am quite, quite certain," he assured her.

"And Edmund—Edmund has given his approval?"

"He even went so far as to say he believed I could make you happy." He cupped her face between his hands. "And I will make you happy, Kate. I promise you I will."

Catriona closed her eyes and felt his mouth come down on hers. It was far from the chaste kiss she was certain Margaret and Mr. Halley had exchanged, but Catriona, far from objecting, clung to him. After a few minutes he moved her to the sofa and began to kiss her again. Catriona responded to him passionately. She would blot Edmund out of her mind, she thought. She would forget him in the arms of the marquis. She would *make* herself forget him.

"Christ, Kate." The marquis's voice sounded strangely husky. He put her away from him. Catriona was surprised to notice that he was trembling. "Your cousin said you don't fully recognize your own power of provocation. He was right."

Catriona drew a little away from him. "I

don't even know your name," she said after a minute.

"It's Richard, my little love."

"Richard!" She smiled, suddenly delighted. "That was my father's name."

"Clearly a good omen." His voice was sounding more normal. "You must come down and see Monkleigh Abbey, my home. I think you'll like it."

"I'm sure I shall." She looked up into his blue eyes, which were smiling at her so tenderly, and said impulsively, "Let's have a dozen children, Richard! Wouldn't it be fun?"

He cleared his throat. "Actually, it would be. I rather like children."

She grinned at him. "From a former rake and confirmed bachelor, this is very astonishing talk."

"From now on I can promise you one thing," he said, and there was an odd gravity in his voice and face, "there will be room in my life for only one woman. You."

Again Catriona felt that brief stab of fear. She hadn't realized she was so important to him. "That's very reassuring," she said after a minute. And then, because she felt grateful to him and because she did not want to hurt him, she added, "I love you, Richard."

After the marquis left, Catriona sat by herself in the morning room for a few minutes. She was not quite sure if she had done the right thing. She sighed, looked up, and there was Edmund in the doorway. "Oh," she said and stared at him.

He moved slowly into the room, and her heart contracted a little as she watched him. He sat down in a chair near her and said calmly, "So you are to be the Marchioness of Hampton."

"I—I suppose I am," replied Catriona in a small voice.

"You liked him right from the start, didn't you?" said Edmund.

"Yes. At first he was attractive because he was a rebel, but then I liked him for himself."

"A rebel." Edmund gazed at her out of inscrutable dark eyes. "Of course, that's what it was."

Catriona grimaced. "I'm a bit of a rebel myself, as you well know."

"More than a bit, I'd say." She smiled a little and he went on, "What else do you like about him?"

"His sense of humor," she replied promptly. "He's the sort of person whose eye you can catch to share a private joke." She swallowed and added, conscious of venturing into dangerous waters, "In that way he's like you."

Edmund didn't seem to hear her. "He loves you," he said after a minute.

"Yes, I believe he does." She laughed a little nervously. "I don't know why. I've done nothing to deserve it."

"Do you love him?"

It was the one question she had feared. She braced herself and said clearly, "Yes."

There was a long silence, during which she did not dare to look at him. When finally she did look up from her lap, it was to find him staring into the empty grate of the fireplace. His head was outlined against the pale gold of the wing-backed chair he was sitting in. Then he turned, and she was caught and held by the large, luminous eyes that always looked so startling in the austere masculinity of his face. "Good," he said. "You, of all people, should not marry where you do not love."

And she knew suddenly that this was true. She should not marry the marquis. She would never feel for him, she would never feel for anyone else in the world, what she felt for Edmund. The mere flicker of his eyelash meant more to her, did more to her, than the marquis's most passionate kisses.

She dragged her eyes away from Edmund's face. But what am I to do? she thought wildly. For a brief minute she hovered on the brink of throwing herself at him and confessing everything. She would beg him not to send her away, beg him to let her stay with him. And then he rose to his feet.

"I believe he will make you a good husband, Catriona." He smiled at her. "They say reformed rakes do."

The moment was gone. Catriona rose as well. "Do they?" she asked tonelessly. "Well, we shall see, won't we?"

"He had better," said Edmund with totally unexpected violence, "or I'll murder him."

Catriona stared in astonishment as on that note her cousin left the room.

Chapter Eighteen

Catriona did not leave but sat down again and stared at the gold wing chair that only moments ago had held Edmund. "He will make you a good husband," Edmund had said, and Catriona thought that probably he would. A better husband than Edmund, with his complicated personality, his temper, his "tunnels."

The problem was that it was Edmund she loved.

Very slowly Catriona rose from the sofa. She went upstairs like a sleepwalker and told her news to Meg and Cousin Henrietta. She smiled at their good wishes and talked to Meg about wedding plans. And all the time she felt as if her heart were breaking.

The announcement of both Catriona's and Margaret's engagements appeared in the *Post* the following day. Margaret's news caused little stir. It was a not unexpected development between two pleasant but not extraordinary people. The ton was agog, however, over Catriona and the marquis. He had been given up as a lost cause years ago. No one had dreamed that now at the age of thirty-four he would be caught by a seventeen-year-old chit just out of the schoolroom.

"It's really comical," Catriona told him as they drove in the park a few afternoons after the announcement. "I feel as if I should be wearing your scalp at my belt, as the red Indians do in America, as a sign of conquest. I had no idea you were such a catch."

He was handling the reins with easy expertise and turned his head a minute to smile down at her. "You thought, in fact, that you were rescuing me from the social dustbin."

She laughed. "I did. Isn't that terrible?"

"Not at all. It was quite understandable. Fond mamas kept their daughters away from me because they did not trust me to marry them. If they had thought I was inclined to marriage, however, I should have been welcomed with open arms." He looked cynical. "I'm very rich, my dear. That covers a multitude of sins."

"Are you really rich?" Catriona asked curiously.

"I am." He glanced at her again, an intriguing glint of blue. "I won a fortune at the gaming table."

Catriona frowned. "Do you still gamble?"

"Yes." He smiled. "But not for fortunes."

Catriona's frown smoothed out. "Good. It would be very disagreeable to lose all that money once you had grown accustomed to having it."

"Will you like being rich?" He was paying close attention now to his horses.

"Yes," said Catriona positively. "I was very poor when I was a child, you see, and so I know that being rich is better. When you're poor, you are helpless. When you're rich, you can keep your land in good heart, you can repair your tenants' cottages, you can assist the poor and needy in your neighborhood." She sat up straighter. "You can buy cows and sheep. You can employ people in your house and gardens and stables, you can . . ." She broke off as he pulled the phaeton to a halt and looked at him in surprise. "Why are you stopping, Richard?"

"You never cease to astonish me, Kate," he said softly.

She looked extremely puzzled. "I don't see why. What I've just said is plain common sense, surely."

He started the horses again. "I suppose it is," he said in an odd voice. There was a phaeton coming toward them. "Here are your cousin and Lady Sophia," he commented as the two carriages approached each other. The marquis pulled up, and Edmund did likewise. The two couples exchanged pleasantries for a minute, and Catriona stared, she hoped unobtrusively, at Sophia.

There was no denying the other girl's beauty. But there was a coldness about those chiseled classical features that repelled Catriona. There was not the slightest hint of humor in Sophia's celestial-blue eyes.

"Do you like Lady Sophia?" Catriona asked the marquis after they had resumed their drive.

"She scares me to death," he replied promptly.

"Me too," said Catriona fervently. "She's so—chilly."

He grinned. "They call her the ice maiden in the clubs."

"Do they?" She looked at him speculatively. "And what do they call me?"

He put a hand briefly over hers as they lay folded together in her lap. "Very shortly they will call you my wife," he said softly. And smiled at her.

Catriona felt a flicker of guilt. It wasn't right that he should be so happy at the thought of marrying her. She would be a good wife to him, she told herself. She would see to it that he never guessed the truth. She smiled back, and for a brief second his hand tightened on hers. Then he turned back to his horses.

Catriona and Margaret were both to be married in the autumn. In the meantime Catriona was introduced to the marquis's sister, Lady Louisa Hartley, who was a good deal older than her brother. She was his only close relative and appeared to be mildly pleased with the prospect of his upcoming marriage.

"I suppose she would have been happier with someone far grander than I," Catriona commented shrewdly to Margaret, "but she's so pleased to see him being dragged to the altar that she isn't going to be too fussy."

"I wouldn't say Lord Hampton is being dragged to the altar," Margaret replied gently. "I should say rather it was the other way around."

"What do you mean?" asked Catriona cautiously.

"I mean that you're not happy, Kate. And that I'm worried about you."

"Why do you say that I'm not happy?"

"Because I know you too well. Oh, I daresay you've fooled everyone else. But I shared a nursery with you for seven years. Remember?"

Catriona bent her head. "Yes."

"Don't you love Lord Hampton, Kate?"

"No." Catriona looked up at Margaret, and her eyes were very bright. "I like him very much, Meg. I like him better than anyone I've met in London. I want to love him."

"I see." Margaret looked at Catriona, and her gentle, pretty face was very sober. "Do you feel you have to get married, Kate? Because of Edmund?"

Catriona felt her heart give one great jolt. Her nails dug into her palms. "What do you mean?" she breathed.

"Well, it looks as if Edmund is going to marry Sophia Heatherstone. Do you feel obligated to remove yourself from Evesham? You shouldn't, you know. Edmund would be extremely upset if he thought you were marrying only to make things easy for him. You know how he loves you."

"Yes," said Catriona hollowly. "I know."

"I don't mean to pry," Margaret said apologetically, "but I am in love, and so I noticed."

"You aren't prying," Catriona assured her. "I think that for me love will come after marriage."

Margaret's eyes dropped. "Aren't you—aren't you a little nervous about marriage, Kate? About the physical part, I mean?"

"No," said Catriona truthfully if immodestly. "I rather think that's the part I'm going to like best."

Margaret was not the only one who noticed Catriona's restraint. The marquis too was conscious of a shadow that sometimes seemed to lay between them. He was beginning to be aware that he had not penetrated Catriona's deepest feelings and he was beginning to wonder as well if there was someone else who had. At unexpected moments she would freeze on him, and the unknown shadow would cloud the easy communication they usually shared. He couldn't pin it down and he tried to tell himself he was mistaken. He hoped that marriage would drive the shadow away once and for all. Once she was truly his, once he was able to show her what love between a man and a woman could be, then, he thought, then she would be wholly his. For now he contented himself with wooing her with all the considerable charm and experience he had accumulated in a notably successful career.

And Catriona responded. She did like the marquis and she knew she would like making love with him. But she did not feel that dizzy wildness that the very thought of Edmund conjured up in her. She would settle down with Richard and have children and try very hard to find a measure of content. But ecstasy would always elude her. For her ecstasy would always lie in the arms of Edmund not in the arms of her husband.

Chapter Nineteen

The betting in the clubs was running high that the Duke of Burford would offer for Lady Sophia Heatherstone. It would be a very suitable match. Lady Dawley talked as if it was almost a settled thing. It was only his grandmother who ventured a note of disapproval, and that to Catriona and not to Edmund.

"Do you like Lady Sophia, Kate?" the duchess asked, unconsciously echoing Catriona's question to the marquis.

"No," said Catriona uncompromisingly. "I think she is a cold fish."

The duchess sighed. "I fear you are right, my dear. And I do not think she is the right girl for Edmund. She will encourage all the wrong aspects of his character."

"She'll drive him into a permanent tunnel," Catriona prophesied gloomily.

"He doesn't love her," the duchess said. "I can see no sign of that. He is simply fulfilling his duty, and from an objective point of view I suppose Lady Sophia is extremely appropriate. She is beautiful and well born and elegant."

"A cold fish," Catriona repeated.

"Yes." The duchess sighed again. "And an inflexible moralist, I fear. If he marries her, all the side of Edmund that is warm and spontaneous will be blighted."

"Why don't you talk to him, Grandmama?"

"There are some things, Kate, that one simply cannot talk to Edmund about. And lately he has been more unapproachable than usual." The duchess smiled at Catriona. "You have always been the one Edmund unbends with, my dear."

Catriona's throat was suddenly tight and aching. "Well, I cannot talk to him about Lady Sophia, Grandmama."

"Of course you cannot," the duchess said quickly. "I never thought of such a thing." She patted Catriona's hand. "I'm just an old woman who needed someone to talk to. And you have a talent for attracting people who are in distress."

"Anyway," Catriona said with even greater gloom than before, "he may love her. She is certainly the most beautiful girl I've ever seen. Men are swayed by things like that."

The duchess smothered a smile. "Yes," she said. "They are."

Catriona rose to her feet. "But she's a cold

fish all the same," she repeated again before she went off to join Margaret on an expedition to Bond Street.

There was a very elegant ball at the Bridgewaters a few days after Catriona's conversation with the duchess, and the inhabitants of Burford House attended en masse along with the Marquis of Hampton and Mr. Halley. Catriona was dancing with the marquis when she looked toward the French windows and saw Edmund standing next to a woman she had never seen before. Catriona stared.

"Who is that talking to Edmund?" she asked the marquis in hushed tones.

He looked. "That is the Countess of Lochaber. She used to be Frances Stewart," he added, as if that should explain everything.

"Oh," said Catriona and kept on staring. The name of Frances Stewart was legendary. The story of her come-out was repeated diligently every year into the ears of aspiring debutantes. She had turned down an array of blue-blooded, wealthy and noble suitors and eventually had married an impoverished Scottish earl and buried herself in the Highlands. Catriona looked at the very tall, very dark man who was standing on Lady Lochaber's other side and decided he must be her husband.

When the dance ended, Catriona and the marquis moved to join Edmund. Frances Lochaber, Catriona decided, as they were introduced and the countess smiled at her warmly, made

Sophia Heatherstone look plain. Frances was fair, like Sophia, but her miraculous hair was so pale that it looked silver rather than gold. She had a hauntingly beautiful face, which was not cold-looking at all. Quite the contrary. The green eyes that were smiling at Catriona held both warmth and friendliness. She was quite tall and slender; Catriona had to look up at her.

"How nice to meet you, Miss MacIan," she was saying. "We've only been in London for a few days, and already my husband is longing for a fellow Scot to talk to. You must let me introduce you." She turned and put her hand on the arm of the very tall man, whose attention had been claimed by Mrs. Mason-Burgley. "Ian," she said gently, "come and meet Catriona MacIan."

"Catriona!" said a very deep voice. "What is a girl named Catriona doing in a place like London?"

"Going to dances, for one thing," Catriona replied and looked way up into a face as dark and as vivid with life as her own.

Ian Macdonald grinned and raised a black eyebrow. "You're a long way from Ardnamurchan," he said to her in Gaelic.

Catriona frowned and thought for a minute. "Not in my heart," she answered finally, haltingly, in the same language, and saw approval in the man's dark eyes.

The Lochabers, it appeared, had come south to bring Frances's daughter, Nell, to spend a

few weeks with her grandparents. Before
Frances had married the Earl of Lochaber, she
had been married to Lord Robert Sedburgh, the
eldest son of the Earl and Countess of Aysgarth,
and she had had a daughter by him before he
died. The Lochabers also had a baby son, whom
they had left at home in Scotland under the
care of his grandmother, the dowager Countess
of Lochaber.

"How old is your baby?" Catriona asked eagerly when this piece of information came out.
She had become quite interested in babies
recently.

"Just a year," Frances replied with a smile.
"And he's an absolute demon." Her long green
eyes glinted briefly. "Just like his father," she
said and looked briefly at her husband, who
was now deep in conversation with Edmund.

"I didn't realize the duke and Lord Lochaber
knew each other," commented the marquis. He
smiled a little at Frances. "You must admit
they're hardly alike."

"They were great friends at school," Frances
said, and the marquis looked even more surprised.

"Hampton can't understand how you ever
came to notice a scapegrace like myself, Burford." Ian Macdonald's deep voice sounded distinctly amused as he and Edmund moved to
join the larger circle.

"Notice you?" said Edmund coolly. "It was
impossible not to notice you. You pretty well
ran Eton while you were there." Suddenly his

face relaxed into its rare, warm smile. "You made a bit of a noise at Cambridge too, as I recall."

"Oh," said Catriona innocently, "were you a scholar too, Lord Lochaber?" The whole circle broke up into laughter, and Catriona stared with good-natured bewilderment into Ian's dark eyes.

"The only thing Ian ever studied at Cambridge," said Lord Lochaber's loving wife with distinct tartness, "was how to make an idiot of himself."

"True," said Edmund gravely. "But he did it on such a grand scale that it was quite impressive."

"You weren't a scholar, then, like Edmund?" asked Catriona.

"She'll pin you to the wall every time, Lochaber," Edmund murmured, and Ian grinned.

"I put in three wretched years at Cambridge, Miss MacIan, and then I decided I had had enough. Unfortunately, my family"—and here the dark eyes briefly touched the lovely face of his wife—"wanted me to stay. So I had to get thrown out. Which I did."

"I know," put in Mr. Halley unexpectedly. "I heard about it when I was up at Cambridge. Everybody always hears about it," he added naively.

"Goodness, what did you do?" asked Catriona, wide-eyed.

Edmund grinned. "To the wall," he said and laughed.

Ian's strong, masculine face abruptly lit with an answering smile. For a brief minute they looked strangely alike. "Everyone always blamed me for that race," Ian said softly. " 'Only Ian Macdonald could have thought up that escapade.' That's what they all said. When the truth is . . ." He broke off tantalizingly, and everyone stared at him. He was right. He had the kind of face that one could believe anything of. Next to him Edmund looked very polished, very elegant, very civilized. Catriona saw her cousin's eyes and suddenly laughed.

"It was Edmund's idea!" she cried.

"It was indeed," Ian said. "I'm glad to see there's someone else who isn't fooled by you, Burford."

"You were a bad influence on me," Edmund said smoothly.

"Hah!" said Ian. "You plotted it all out, cool and calculating, with that mathematical precision you were so famous for. All I did was listen."

"And drink."

"And drink. Of course."

"And do it."

"True."

"But didn't you race, Edmund?" asked Catriona.

"Of course. But *I* didn't get caught."

"You didn't want to get thrown out."

"Very true. Speaking of drinks, Lochaber . . ."

"Lead the way," said Ian, and the two of them ambled off, still talking.

"I rather suspect they are both a bad influence," said Frances Lochaber with amusement. "Ian was so disappointed last year when we were in London and the duke was away in Paris. He's always said Burford was the only Englishman he ever really liked."

"I wonder why Lord Lochaber never came to visit at Evesham," said Catriona.

"He was fighting in South America until just a year ago," Frances replied quietly. "He left right after that famous scene they were both discussing just now."

"Oh," said Catriona. For a minute the two women watched the black heads of Edmund and Ian as they made their way across the room, then Catriona turned to ask Frances something else, but suddenly it seemed as if they were surrounded. Catriona watched for a minute as Frances responded expertly and charmingly to the flock of male admirers who had descended upon her, then the marquis spoke into her ear.

"Shall we dance?"

"Yes." Catriona smiled up at him with great sweetness. "Please, Richard, I should very much like to dance."

She danced with the marquis and then with several other men and she was standing again with her fiancé when Lord Lochaber came up and said, "You won't deny me a turn with a fellow Scot, will you, Hampton?"

"Of course not," answered the marquis and watched Catriona glide off with Ian in a waltz before heading toward the excellent champagne.

"What were you and Edmund talking about for so long?" Catriona asked almost immediately. She looked around and saw Edmund dancing with Frances Lochaber.

"Sheep," said Ian in response to her question.

"Do you have sheep?" asked Catriona. "Edmund has a great number of them."

"I know. I'm new in the sheep business, but his family has been in it for centuries. He's going to be very helpful to me."

"Is he?" Catriona smiled up at him. He was even taller than Edmund. "I'm glad," she said.

He smiled back, and she was aware suddenly of his potent attractiveness. He was not precisely handsome. It was the impression of intense life contained in his high-cheekboned face that was so beguiling. She did not realize that what she was seeing in Ian's face was a mirror image of her own extraordinary magnetism.

Frances Lochaber realized it. "Look at them," she said softly to Edmund, and obediently he turned his head to watch Catriona and Ian. "The Celts," said Frances. "What quality is there in the race that makes them burn so much brighter than anyone else?"

"I don't know," answered Edmund quietly.

"You ought to have Catriona's portrait painted," Frances said. "Perhaps Ian's cousin Douglas would do it."

"That will be for her husband to arrange," Edmund said stiffly after a minute.

"Yes," said Frances. "I suppose so. How much older Lord Rivers is looking these days," she remarked then, tactfully changing the subject.

"I don't believe he is well," Edmund replied, smoothly following her lead. And for the remainder of their dance they spoke only trivial pleasantries. It was a game they were both experts in.

Chapter Twenty

Edmund and Ian were inseparable for the next few days, and Catriona found herself spending a good deal of time in the company of Ian's wife. Frances said she had come to London to shop, and since Catriona was in the process of putting together a trousseau, she lent Frances her company on numerous excursions.

"It's so much more fun to shop with someone," Frances confided. "And I never have made friends with many Englishwomen. They always seem so cold."

Catriona grinned. "I can't imagine why."

"And Ian is impossible to shop with," Frances went on serenely. "I could choose the most hideous dress imaginable, and he'd say it looked fine. I'm so glad the duke is keeping him busy. Otherwise, I'm afraid, he'd be ready to descend on Aysgarth right now and snatch Nell back so we could go home. And her grandparents so look forward to seeing her. It would be a shame to give them less than a month."

The marquis was not bored by shopping and he accompanied them on a number of expeditions. He also arranged an outing to Richmond Park for the three of them, Margaret, Mr. Halley, and Lord Morton, one of Frances's seemingly unending stream of admirers. At the last minute their party was joined by Edmund and Ian, quite throwing the numbers off, as Frances complained to her husband when he appeared dressed in buckskins and riding boots.

"I thought I had better start keeping a closer eye on you," he returned imperturbably. "Haven't any of your old suitors gotten married?"

"Certainly they have." She smiled up at him. "They're no longer suitors; they're friends."

"So you say." He put his hands on her waist and lifted her easily into the saddle. She looked down into his upturned dark face, and her smile was ineffably lovely. He had never had any cause to be jealous of her, and he knew it.

"Yes," she said softly. "So I say. But I am not so sanguine about my own rivals."

His hands were still on her waist. "What rivals?" he asked in surprise.

"The Duke of Burford," she answered smartly, "and his sheep." She touched her heel to her horse's side and walked sedately away down the street.

In two minutes Ian had caught up with her. "Today," he said, "I will be a devoted husband." She glanced up at him and saw the faint amusement in his dark eyes. "Neither Morton nor Hampton will get near you," he promised.

"Lord Hampton is not interested in me," his wife said.

"No, that's true; he's not." Ian grinned. "She's a captivating little minx, isn't she?"

"Yes," said Frances, and there was no answering smile in her voice. "I only hope she's chosen the right man."

There was no more time for conversation. They had reached Grosvenor Square, where they were to meet the rest of the party. The ride to Richmond was uneventful. It was a lovely day, and once they got inside the gates of the park, they all allowed their horses to stretch out into a gallop. Margaret and Mr. Halley were the first to slow down, and then Frances expertly brought her own horse down to a trot and then a walk. She was joined in a minute by the duke. Catriona, the marquis, and the rest galloped on ahead.

"How have you been enjoying your stay in London, Lady Lochaber?" Edmund asked civilly as his horse fell in next to hers.

"Very much. As I expect you know, Catriona and I have been shopping. There are no shops like London's in Edinburgh—although you cannot get Ian to admit that."

Edmund laughed. "He's always been a fiercely proud Scot."

"Yes. So am I, actually," Frances added.

Edmund looked at her in surprise. "That's right. You are Scottish as well, aren't you?"

"One hundred percent. Although Catriona, who is only half-Scot, is more a Celt than I. I show the Scandinavian blood of the western isles."

Edmund appeared interested and began to ask her some questions about Scottish history. Frances answered him, and they rode together for perhaps ten minutes, engrossed in conversation. But Frances, who had an extremely feminine and perceptive nature, knew instinctively that Edmund was not interested in her. The spark that was so frequently present in men's eyes when they looked at her was not there in his. He was in love with someone, she guessed shrewdly, so in love that he scarcely noticed her own beauty; or rather, he noticed— he was not blind—but he was not moved by it. It happened that way with some men when they were totally involved with one woman. She knew. It was like that for Ian. Frances wondered idly who it was for the duke.

She asked Catriona as the two of them rode together on the way home. Ian and the duke were riding ahead with Margaret and Mr. Halley, and Lord Hampton and Lord Morton had gotten into a conversation about a pair of horses they were both interested in.

"Is your cousin going to be married?" Frances asked Catriona in a soft voice.

"I'm afraid so," came the glum reply. "To Lady Sophia Heatherstone."

"What! That cold fish!" Frances looked appalled.

"Isn't she awful?" Catriona said with passion. "I used to tell myself it was because she was so beautiful that he liked her. But next to you she's not beautiful at all."

"Or next to you," said Frances.

"Me?"

"Yes, you. Don't look so surprised. You know the effect you have on men."

Catriona kept her eyes on her horse's ears. "I'm beginning to," she muttered. "It's a little frightening. I never thought I was pretty."

"You're not pretty. Nor is Ian handsome. But he'd have to beat the women off with a stick if I weren't around to put up a No Trespassing sign."

"Yes," said Catriona, recalling her dance with the Earl of Lochaber. "He would."

"It's the same thing you have," said Frances. "The thing that what's-her-name Heatherstone does not have."

"Sophia," said Catriona. "Her name's Sophia. I *hate* the name Sophia."

"It's never been a favorite of mine either."

"Kate!" called the marquis. "Would you like a matched pair of grays?" Catriona dutifully slowed her horse to turn and answer him.

*   *   *

They were starving when they got back to Burford House, and the duke invited them to stay for a cold supper. "We're all in riding clothes," he said easily, "so it won't matter."

Frances went upstairs with Catriona and Margaret to tidy up. She spent quite a long time arranging her hair, and Catriona finally said to Margaret, "You go ahead, Meg. I'll wait for Lady Lochaber." Margaret was anxious to get back to Mr. Halley and gave Catriona a grateful look before departing.

Frances ran the comb one more time through her ash-blond curls and turned to look at Catriona. "How old are you, Catriona?" she asked softly.

"Seventeen. I'll be eighteen in the fall."

Frances sighed. "Eighteen," she said. "When I was eighteen, I made the biggest mistake of my whole life."

Catriona's eyes enlarged. "What was that?"

"I married a man I didn't love."

Catriona felt color staining her cheeks. "Oh," she said.

"He was a wonderful man and he loved me very much. I felt constantly guilty that I couldn't love him as he deserved." She scanned Catriona's face. "I had quarreled with Ian, you see, and he went off to South America."

"Oh," said Catriona again. She felt incapable of finding any other word.

"I've never discussed my first marriage with anyone," Frances said, "and I suppose you wonder why I'm telling you this now. . . ." She broke off as Catriona shook her head.

"I think I know why." Her voice sounded very gruff.

"I don't want to pry." Frances was speaking very slowly now. "I realize you scarcely know me, and it is extremely presumptuous on my part to try to give you advice, but I would hate to see you make the same mistake I did."

Catriona sat down. It was a relief to have someone to talk to, someone older and more mature than she. "I want to love Richard," she said earnestly. "I like him very much."

"It would be hard not to," answered Frances. "He is charming. But you can't will yourself to love someone, Catriona. It doesn't work." She smiled ruefully. "I know, believe me."

"But everything turned out all right for you."

"Yes." There was a shadow of strain around Frances's lovely eyes. "Because Rob died."

"Yes," Catriona almost whispered. "I see."

"Sometimes I ask myself what I would have done if I had been married to Rob and Ian came back. And then I think, God, I'm glad Rob died. And he was such a good man, Catriona. He was so good to me." Frances's face looked almost haunted. "Don't do it, Catriona. One day you will really fall in love, and then it will be hell."

"Have you always loved Ian?"

"There's never been anyone else for me. There never will be."

"I know." Catriona bowed her head. "I *know*. But Ian loved you back."

"Yes." Frances looked at Catriona's shining dark head. She was beginning to understand the problem.

"I have to get married, don't you see?" Catriona was going on recklessly. "I have to get away from Edmund. I can't live in the same house with him if he is married to Sophia Heatherstone."

"Yes," Frances said very slowly. "Yes, I believe I do see."

Catriona looked up. "What shall I do?"

Frances's beautiful face looked very preoccupied. "The duke is not engaged as yet, is he?"

"No."

"Are you quite sure he plans to become engaged?"

"Everyone seems to think he will."

Frances smiled in faint irony. "That means exactly nothing. Let me think about this for a few days."

"You won't tell Lord Lochaber?" Catriona asked anxiously.

"Good God, no," Frances answered instantly. "He'd be furious with me for interfering."

"You haven't interfered," Catriona said with a grateful smile.

Frances still looked preoccupied. "Not yet," she said enigmatically and rose to her feet. "We'd better go downstairs. Margaret will be convinced that I'm the vainest creature that ever lived."

"No, she won't," returned Catriona absently. They left the room together, each absorbed in her own thoughts.

Chapter Twenty-one

A week later Catriona left London for Evesham Castle. Edmund had invited the Lochabers, and Frances asked Catriona to come also as company for her. "I can't bear the thought of listening to nothing but sheep talk for a week," she complained.

Ian, who knew his wife could converse very intelligently about sheep and the price of wool, looked at her speculatively. Frances looked back so sweetly that he knew something was brewing, but he hadn't a clue as to what it was.

So Catriona accompanied the Lochabers and Edmund to Evesham. And of course where Catriona went, the Marquis of Hampton went as well. The duchess announced that she was tired of London and wanted to go home. And Lady Dawley decided to go on a visit to her daughter, who had a house full of sick children and needed help. That meant that Margaret would be left without a chaperone, and so she returned to Evesham with the duchess. With Margaret, naturally, came Mr. Halley. And when they reached the Castle, George and Henry were home from school.

Consequently it was a far larger house party than Edmund had envisioned. "Now I've got to think up some schemes to entertain this crowd," he grumbled to Ian before they left London. "I was only planning to show you the estate."

"They don't need to be entertained," Ian said carelessly. "The lovebirds will keep each other occupied. And Frances can come with us."

"I rather got the impression that Lady Lochaber was not looking forward to a week of rusticating."

"Nonsense," said Ian. "There's nothing she likes better than to be outdoors." Edmund said nothing but raised a skeptical eyebrow. Ian's mouth quirked. "I know. I know what she looks like. But she grew up in the Highlands, remember, and she's as strong as a lioness. At home she knows the name of every crofter in Lochaber. And she knows as much about sheep as I do. Don't let her face put you off."

Edmund's large gray eyes suddenly sparkled. "I doubt if Lady Lochaber's face ever put anyone off," he said.

Ian grinned. "True. It's a great trial to me."

"I'm sure it is," returned Edmund drily. And Ian laughed.

*   *   *

As the days went by, Catriona became more and more unhappy. Being at Evesham only made it worse. The marquis was very deeply in love with her; she realized that more clearly with each passing day. And the realization, instead of reassuring her, only added to her wretchedness. She had let him think that she loved him quite as much as he loved her and she felt herself in an increasingly false position. She remembered what Frances had said about feeling guilty all the time and she perfectly understood.

Richard didn't belong at Evesham. She felt oppressed by his presence, his natural assumption of his right to be with her. But she didn't want him. Evesham belonged to her and to Edmund. Richard was an intruder. It was a terrible way to feel about the man you were going to marry.

And then there was George. He acted as if she had betrayed him by becoming engaged. They had had one very uncomfortable scene, and since then he had gone around glaring with open hostility at the marquis. Richard appeared to find him amusing.

"George doesn't know many other girls and so he's fancied himself in love with me," she explained to her fiancé one afternoon after her cousin had been particularly obnoxious. "I've never done anything to encourage him." She felt a pang of conscience and resolutely squashed the memory of a kiss.

The marquis took her hand. They were sitting together in the garden; George had just gone stalking into the house after Lord Hampton had given him a gentle set-down.

"I know, darling," he said. "It's not your fault. It's the sort of thing that's going to happen to you all your life, and if I let it bother me, we shall both be miserable. I shall just have to take a leaf out of Lochaber's book."

She kept her eyes on their clasped hands. "He trusts Frances," she said. "He knows she loves him."

He raised her hand to his lips. "And I trust you."

She looked up into his smiling blue eyes and felt the now familiar pang of guilt. "Richard," she said and stopped. What could she say?

"And you love me," he went on, the smile in his eyes turning to something else.

He was so sweet, Catriona thought. He would take care of her, protect her from herself. "Yes," she said. "Of course I love you." And she let him pull her into his arms.

Edmund, contrary to Lord Lochaber's advice, did arrange a few entertainments for the benefit of his guests. One of his schemes was a picnic on the shore of the very pretty lake that was one of the features of the Castle's park. There were two boats available for those who wanted to go out on the water, and a picturesque walk through the woods and across a small waterfall for those who enjoyed quiet and lovely scenery. There was also a very substantial lunch-eon provided by Gaston, the duke's French cook.

It was a very warm June day, and Catriona had awakened with a slight headache which the heat was not improving. She felt out of sorts, and her usually good temper was sorely tried by the high spirits of all her companions. All she wanted, she thought fretfully as George teased her to go out in a boat and Richard urged her to come for a walk, was to be let alone. She ate too much lunch, which made her feel worse.

Everyone was still sitting on the rugs the duke had provided against grass stains when Catriona got up restlessly and went down to the edge of the water. The sun was hot on her head, and she had a sudden desire to splash her face with cool water. She looked at the picnic group, caught George's eye, and signaled to him. He jumped up immediately and came over to her.

"Would you mind terribly getting me a nap-kin or something, George?" she asked. "I'm so hot. I want to splash some water on my forehead."

"Of course, Kate," he said and moved with alacrity to do her bidding. She smiled at him when he handed her the linen napkin.

"Thank you." She bent down and dipped the napkin in the lake water. It felt very cool and wet against her hot skin. "That feels marvelous."

She handed the napkin to George. "Do you want to try it?"

"Yes." His fingers shook slightly as he took the wet linen from her hand and laid it against his face.

There was a bustle of activity behind them. Margaret and Mr. Halley were going back to the waterfall. Ian wanted to walk around the lake, and after receiving a meaningful glance from Edmund, George offered to go with him and show him the path.

Frances said quite firmly, "Good-bye. I'll see you later," and her husband laughed and went off without her.

Silence fell among the four who were left at the picnic site, then Frances said sweetly, "I should so love to go out in one of those darling boats. Would you row me, Lord Hampton?"

The marquis looked a little surprised, but good manners made him say, "Of course, Lady Lochaber. It will be a pleasure." The two of them got up and went down to the lakeside.

They were well out on the water when Edmund turned to Catriona. "It would be a kindness," he said acidly, "if you would refrain from tormenting poor George."

Her eyes widened. "I? Tormenting George? Whatever do you mean?"

"You know perfectly well what I mean," he answered furiously. "He isn't your pet errand boy, and you oughtn't to exploit his infatuation the way you do."

Her head was beginning to pound. She went

very pale. "Don't dare speak to me like that," she said, quite as furious as he.

"You aren't married yet," he responded. He had opened the neck of his shirt against the heat, and above the crisp white cotton his pulse was beating very fast. "You are still under my charge. And if I see you behaving like a—a heartless flirt—then I'll damn well tell you about it."

"If that's the way you think of me, then I can't wait to get married and away from here." Her voice was shaking with hurt and with temper. "I don't even want to talk to you," she said and lay back on the rug and shut her eyes.

The sun was shining directly on her, and she threw an arm across her eyes to protect them. She could feel perspiration forming on her forehead and upper lip. Her thin dress was sticking to her body. After a few minutes she opened her eyes a slit and looked at Edmund under the protection of her arm.

He was staring at her, and the look in his eyes made her stomach suddenly clench. It was an expression she had come to know well in the last few months, but she had never dreamed of seeing it on Edmund's face. At least not for her. But it was there, and she knew what it meant. Catriona shut her eyes again. Her heart was pounding so hard that she was sure he could hear it. She stayed as still as she could for another minute and then slowly lowered her arm. Edmund was looking at the water, and all she could see of him was his exceedingly aristocratic profile. She ran her tongue across her lips to moisten them.

"I didn't mean that," she said. "About wanting to get away from here."

"I know." His voice sounded as if it were coming from a great distance. He did not turn to look at her. He seemed as far away from her as the moon. But she had not mistaken the expression on his face. She had seen it too often on Richard's—and on George's as well—to fail to recognize it.

There was the sound of voices coming closer, and then Margaret and Mr. Halley appeared from their walk in the woods. Catriona turned to look at her cousin and felt a pang of envy. Meg looked so uncomplicatedly happy. Catriona looked down at the flowered pattern of her thin muslin dress. Her mind was in a whirl. Edmund, she thought. What could it mean?

"Did you have a nice nap, Kate?" It was the marquis back from his boating excursion with Frances. He sat down next to her on the rug.

"Yes," she said in a low voice. Then, "I've got the most awful headache, Richard. Do you think we could go home?"

He was instantly all sympathy. "Of course, darling. Why didn't you say so earlier?" She smiled at him a little wanly, and he went over to Edmund. They talked together for a few minutes, and Catriona saw Edmund glance at her sharply. Then Richard was back and in a few minutes he had her in his phaeton and they were returning along the path to Evesham Castle. He held the reins in one hand and put an arm around her. She leaned her forehead against his shoulder and closed her eyes.

"What do you think about pushing up our wedding date to next month?" he asked after a few minutes.

She sat up. "Why?"

His mouth curved in a rueful smile. "Because I'm finding this business of being engaged a very great strain."

"Oh," she said. And swallowed. "I don't think Grandmama would like it if we disrupted her plans," she offered after a minute's intensive thought.

The set of his mouth now was grim. "I suppose not."

"It hasn't really been that long an engagement," she said weakly.

"It's been an eternity," he said and stopped his horses. The road was private and shaded by the great beech trees that grew on either side. He turned her face up and began to kiss her.

This was different from the way he had kissed her before. She felt his urgency, his desperation, but could conjure up no rapture of response. It just wasn't there, and there was no longer any way she could fool herself into thinking it would come. After a minute he put her away from him and took up his reins. "That is why I would like to push up the wedding date," he said a little shakily.

"I—I'll talk to Grandmama," was all she could say in reply.

Chapter Twenty-two

Once they had got back to Evesham, Catriona pleaded her headache and went up to her room to lie down. Her mind was in a whirl from which a single thought stood out clearly. Edmund did not regard her as a little sister. One did not look at one's little sister the way he had looked at her this afternoon.

He wanted her. What she had seen on his face had been desire, pure and simple. Why, then, had he never given her any indication, why had he allowed her to become engaged to Richard?

Because he couldn't marry her. The answer too was pure and simple. Catriona had never been more conscious of her illegitimacy. Richard had overlooked it, but Richard was not the Duke of Burford. Edmund's position was very

different from Richard's; that had been made
clear to Catriona during these last months.
Edmund was almost royalty, and as such he
had a great responsibility to choose a wife
of impeccable background and impeccable behavior. Catriona could boast of neither. And so
Edmund was allowing her to marry the Marquis of Hampton.

And what would happen in the future when
she was protected by Richard's name? What
would happen if the desire she had read on
Edmund's face this afternoon ever came out
into the open?

She would go to him. She knew it instantly,
unequivocally. She would forget her marriage
vows, forget Richard's kindness and love, and
give to Edmund whatever he wanted from her.

I can't marry Richard.

The thought that had been in her mind for
weeks now became now a solid conviction. She
remembered Frances's words, "What would I
have done if I had been married to Rob and Ian
came back?"

She could not marry Richard. But how was
she to tell him? What was she to say? She
went to the window and impatiently looked
out across the drive. She needed to talk to
Frances.

"You've made the right decision," Frances
told her, when Catriona had finally managed
to get her alone and confide her problem. She
had said nothing about Edmund, only that she

had come to the conclusion that she must break her engagement to Richard.

"But how am I to explain?" Catriona almost wailed. "I've given him every reason to believe I'm in love with him."

"You must simply tell him you mistook your feelings," replied Frances serenely.

"But it will hurt him so terribly."

"I daresay it will. It would hurt him a great deal more, however, if he discovered your feelings after you were married."

"I know it would," replied Catriona glumly. "That's why I've got to do it." She sighed. "He asked me today to push up the wedding date."

Frances looked thoughtful. "Now, that might be an opening, Catriona. Tell him you're not sure, now that the wedding is so close. Put him off. Be sweet and apologetic but inflexible. You know."

Catriona realized that she was receiving advice from an expert. She looked at the incomparably lovely face of her friend and nodded. "Yes. I see."

"Put off the marriage indefinitely. And then we shall see what happens."

Dinner that evening was not very pleasant for Catriona. She sat next to Richard and tried to act normally but she was feeling miserably guilty and uncomfortable. The glowing warmth in the marquis's blue eyes when he looked at her only made her more wretched.

She didn't get a chance to talk to Lord

Hampton, because after the men came into the drawing room, Edmund drew her aside. "Come out on the terrace with me for a few moments, Catriona," he said gravely.

She glanced fleetingly up into his face. There wasn't a hint of passion in his cool, composed features. She had a sudden, sinking conviction that she had dreamed the whole episode this afternoon. She had seen on his face what she wanted to see, not what had really been there. "All right," she almost whispered and followed him out the French doors.

The lawn was bathed in moonlight, and Edmund rested his hands on the stone balustrade and gazed out at the white-lit expanse of grass and fountain. She went to stand next to him, and her eyes followed his. "Hampton tells me you desire to be married next month," he said.

Catriona's eyes widened. "I didn't know he was going to speak to you," was all she managed to get out.

"Is it because of what I said to you this afternoon?"

"No!" She looked up at his beautifully etched profile. "No. It was entirely Richard's idea. In fact"—and here she swallowed and her voice dropped—"I'm not sure that I want to marry him at all."

"What!" He swung around to regard her incredulously. "Are you serious?"

She nodded miserably. "Yes, Edmund, I am. I—I mistook my feelings."

"I don't believe I'm hearing this." She winced

at the note in his voice. "Do you realize that that man is desperately in love with you? And that you have been encouraging him for weeks to believe that his feeling is reciprocated?"

"I know. Edmund, I'm most terribly sorry. I thought I did love him. I *wanted* to love him. But I don't. I can't." The last sentence came out on a swallowed sob.

His face was bleak in the moonlight. "I would never have believed this of you, Catriona. I thought your behavior to George was bad, but this is unpardonable."

He was right. Catriona bowed her head and let his words pour over her. Everything he said was true. She was a selfish flirt. She had no thought for the sufferings of others. She was heartless . . . But she was not heartless. Her heart belonged to him, only he didn't want it. He hated her. She was a despicable person. It was all woefully true.

When he finally stopped talking, she looked up out of shimmering green eyes. "I'm sorry," she said. "Should I marry him anyway?"

"God, no!" He spoke so violently that she jumped. "Eventually you'd meet a man you did love, and I have no desire to see you in the middle of a messy scandal." He looked disgusted. "Under those circumstances, I have very little opinion of your ability to remain true to your husband."

He was right again. She was totally worthless, weak, a wretched person. How could she possibly ever have dreamed that Edmund could love her? He saw her only too clearly.

She stared down at her hands on the balustrade, willing the tears not to fall. "What shall I do?" she whispered.

"You'll have to tell him," he said.

Catriona thought of the tenderness in Lord Hampton's blue eyes. "I can't," she said miserably. She looked up at him and sniffed. "Edmund, will you?"

"Oh, no," he said. "You're the one who misled him, you're the one who promised to marry him. Now you're the one who's going to tell him the truth."

"Edmund!" came the duchess's voice from the room behind them. "My dear, Kate doesn't have a shawl. I don't want her to catch cold."

Without a word the duke opened the French doors and stepped back so that Catriona could precede him into the room. She didn't dare look at him as she went by.

"Goodness," said Frances lightly to George as he sat next to her an hour later over tea, "whatever has gotten into the duke?"

"He had a fight with Kate," George said positively. "She's the only one who can make him lose his temper."

"Is that so?" Frances looked thoughtful. "Do you mean that he is never angry with anyone else?" She looked up at George and smiled bewitchingly.

George blinked. His heart belonged to Catriona, but Frances Lochaber was incredible. "No, I don't precisely mean that, Lady Lochaber," he said. "He's certainly gotten angry with me." He went on in a rush of confidence, "In fact, one of the things I hate most in the world is an interview with Edmund when he's caught me out. He can be so—unnerving."

Frances looked at the austere and aristocratic face of her host. "I can imagine so," she said sympathetically.

"He's always so reasonable, do you see, and quiet. That's what makes it so terrible."

"I perfectly understand," Frances assured him.

George grinned. "But Kate drives him mad. The rest of us are all a little in awe of Edmund, but not Kate. Meg told me she called him a hypocrite and a whited sepulcher—*to his face.*" George looked awestruck, and Frances laughed.

"Good for her."

"Kate is capable of anything," George said wistfully and looked over at his cousin.

Frances followed his gaze. Catriona was staring somberly into the fire. The corners of her mouth curved slightly downward in a way that was quite surprisingly erotic. Her eyes were veiled by their outrageously long lashes. Her great grandmother called her name, and she turned, her head moving gracefully on its lovely long neck. Frances leaned back in her own chair and smiled with sweet satisfaction.

Chapter Twenty-three

The next morning the Duke of Burford was joined for his early-morning ride by both the Earl and the Countess of Lochaber. "This is a pleasant surprise," he said to Frances with a charming smile.

"I'm afraid you must think me dreadfully lazy," she returned, "but at home I'm regularly up at seven, I assure you. I've just been taking a little vacation lately."

"Good for you."

"Tell that to Ian," she said and put a hand on her husband's arm as he sat his horse next to hers. "He routed me out mercilessly this morning."

Her fingers pressed meaningfully into her husband's hard forearm, and Ian shot her a long look out of inscrutable eyes. "An early ride will be good for you," he said blandly, and she removed her hand.

"I'm sure you're right." She smiled sweetly, ignoring her husband's speculative look, and allowed her horse to move forward. The two men followed.

Frances enjoyed the ride very much. She also enjoyed the agricultural talk and to Edmund's surprise she proved very knowledgeable. Despite Ian's testimonial, he had had little faith that her knowledge was more than superficial.

Her chance came when they dismounted by one of the sheep pastures. Ian wanted to look more closely at the duke's breed, and they all started off on foot, Frances moving as swiftly and easily as the men. Halfway across the pasture she stopped.

"I'm tired," she complained softly. "Ian, you go ahead and look at the sheep. I'll stay here and wait. Perhaps you would stay with me, Your Grace." She gave Edmund a rueful smile. "Ian doesn't need anyone to explain sheep to him, you know."

Both men stared at her suspiciously. She didn't look remotely tired. She stared limpidly back, and her husband suddenly grinned.

"All right, sweetheart," he said, "have it your way." He turned to move off across the pasture. "I wondered why you wanted to get up so early," he added wickedly over his shoulder as he went.

Frances chuckled, a delicious, deep gurgling sound. "Wretch," she said to her husband's departing back. Then she turned to the duke.

Edmund was not smiling. He also appeared totally unmoved by the sight of her in the brilliant early-morning sunshine. Frances found this very reassuring.

"I want to talk to you about Catriona," she said.

His face went very still. "Oh?"

"Yes. You simply must not allow her to marry Lord Hampton."

"I see." He looked across the field to where Ian had finally joined up with the sheep. "And why not, Lady Lochaber?"

"Well, she is only getting married because she feels it is what you want," Frances said candidly. "And I can't help but feel that it will be a very great mistake."

"What *I* want?" echoed Edmund, astonished. "If I did anything, it was to discourage her from becoming engaged to Hampton. He is so much older and more sophisticated than she."

"You see, she feels she is in your way," Frances explained sadly. "She feels she has to get married, that you expect it of her, and she likes Lord Hampton better than anyone else she met in London."

"That's simply not true." Edmund's voice was very controlled. "My grandmother adores Catriona. She would be happy to have her remain at Evesham forever."

"Perhaps." Frances regarded him thoughtfully. "But Catriona told me also that she simply could not live in the same house as you once you were married."

There was a pinched look about Edmund's aristocratic nostrils. "Why not?" he asked tensely.

Frances looked across the field toward her husband. "Would you like to live with Catriona and her husband?" she asked him back.

The silence next to her was deafening. Frances kept her eyes on the tall, dark man who was now intently regarding the duke's sheep. "I fell in love with Ian when I was twelve years old," she said softly, almost to herself. "I've never loved anyone else. But I made the mistake Catriona will make if she marries Lord Hampton." She tilted her beautiful face to look at him. "Don't let her do that, Your Grace."

Edmund stared at her, and all his cool reserve had vanished. "Are you telling me ..." he began and then broke off.

"Yes," said Frances simply. "I am."

For a long moment Edmund didn't speak. "Would you mind if I left you and Ian, Lady Lochaber? I'd like to get back to the Castle right away."

Frances smiled warmly. "Go right ahead, Your Grace. We know our way home."

"Where the devil is Burford going?" Ian asked his wife as he came up to her a few minutes later.

"He just remembered an urgent errand," Frances answered serenely. Ian didn't say anything. He just regarded her in silence, waiting. She chuckled. "Oh, all right. I told him that Catriona doesn't want to marry Lord Hampton, that she's in love with him."

"Good God," said Ian. "Are you sure of that?"

"Of course. And what's more, the duke is in love with her. Only both of them were afraid to tell the other. A little outside intervention was clearly called for."

Ian looked sardonic. "This is beginning to sound like something out of a very bad play. I hope the devil you're right, Frances. It isn't safe to go meddling in other people's lives."

Her back was very straight. "I knew it. I knew you'd say that. I told Catriona you would. I am not meddling, Ian. I am doing both of them a great service."

Her husband gave an eloquent snort. "All right, I gather Catriona told you how she feels. But how do you know about Burford? You scarcely know him, for God's sake. And he seems damned interested in that blond iceberg we met in London."

Frances glared. "I know how the duke feels because George Talbot told me last night that Catriona was the only person who could make Burford lose his temper."

"Christ," he said. "And because of that totally inane piece of information you have interfered in the lives of two people you scarcely know?"

"Ian Macdonald"—Frances's eyes were greener than the grass that surrounded them—"you are the most colossally stupid and insensitive man I have ever met." And she turned and stalked away toward the horses.

The thick grass muffled her husband's footsteps, and she didn't know he was behind her until his hands encircled her waist. "All right, sweetheart," he said and swung her up into his arms. "I understand."

Frances's eyes softened to sea-green, and she put her arms around his neck. "You should," she said softly.

He began to walk toward the horses, still carrying her easily. "It's time we were getting home," he said. "I'm tired of other people's houses." His dark face was very grave as he looked down at her. "I'm tired of sharing you with half the world."

"Mmm," said Frances. "And I miss my baby." She kissed the strong line of jaw that was close to her face. "We can go down to Aysgarth tomorrow and get Nell."

His arms tightened. "Let's do that."

"All right." And she laid her head on his shoulder.

Edmund asked for Catriona the minute he walked into the house. She was still in her room, he was told. It was, after all, only ten o'clock in the morning.

"Will you have someone ask her to come to the library as soon as it is convenient?" he told his butler. "I will be waiting."

"Very good, Your Grace," Hutchins replied

and went off to tell a maid to relay the message to Miss Catriona.

It was almost half an hour before Catriona appeared in the doorway of the library. "You wanted to see me, Edmund?" she asked nervously. She was certain he was going to insist that she tell Richard right away, and she quailed at the thought.

"Yes. Come in and close the door, Catriona."

He sounded grimmer and grimmer. She closed the door carefully and advanced into the room. "W-what did you want to see me about?"

"I want you to tell me honestly why you agreed to marry Hampton in the first place," he said.

She stared at him in bewilderment. "I thought I loved him," she said faintly.

There was a glimmer in his gray eyes that caught and held her own. Her heart lurched and then began to slam in her chest. "Not according to Lady Lochaber," he said.

"You've been talking to Frances?" she murmured in wonder. The look she had seen on his face yesterday at the lake was back. "Edmund," she said. He stepped closer, and her lips parted. She gazed up at him with her heart in her eyes. *"Edmund."* And then she was in his arms.

Every fiber of her being responded to his kiss. Her arms around his neck, she arched against him, drowning in the sensations his touch awoke in her. She didn't surface until he bent so that her feet touched the ground again and then stepped back from her a little.

"Almighty God," he said. "I can quite see why Hampton wanted to put forward the wedding date." His voice was unsteady, his eyes midnight-black.

Catriona laughed softly and dizzily. "Oh, Edmund," she said. "I love you so much."

"I didn't know." His long fingers traced the line of her cheekbone with delicate precision. "I thought you regarded me as a big brother and I have been trying for months quite desperately to keep you from seeing that my own feelings were not brotherly at all."

"Well, you succeeded only too well." She flashed a brilliant smile. "I've been utterly miserable. I thought you loved Sophia Heatherstone."

"I was trying to cloud the waters." He looked down into her upturned face. "I've been in love with you since you were ten years old. Isn't that a disgraceful thing to admit? Only I didn't realize it until I returned from France in November. You threw yourself into my arms, and it hit me then quite catastrophically that you weren't a little girl any more. I wanted never to let you go."

She laughed. "So that was why you froze up so and seemed to go away from me. I couldn't imagine what I had done to offend you."

"Offend me?" He smiled a little bitterly. "It was I who offended you, sweetheart. I was beastly to you at Christmas, I know that. But you see, I was so terribly jealous."

Catriona's eyes were wide with wonder. Edmund had been jealous of her! So that was why he had been so nasty about George and about Richard. "I wanted to scratch out Sophia Heatherstone's eyes," she admitted. "I got engaged to Richard because I knew I couldn't bear to live in the same house with you once you belonged to another woman. And Richard doesn't live too close to Evesham. I wouldn't have had to see you very often." She heaved a sigh. "Oh, Edmund, I've been so terribly, terribly unhappy!"

His arms came around her again, and she was pulled hard against his chest. "You're never going to be unhappy again. I'm going to see to that." He sounded fierce.

Catriona closed her eyes, melting into his embrace, her mouth soft and responsive under his.

"I appear to be interrupting," came a voice behind her, and Catriona felt Edmund stiffen. It was a few seconds before she recognized the marquis's voice. She froze and then in abject cowardice turned her face into Edmund's shoulder and left him to handle it.

Edmund kept an arm firmly around her and looked at the marquis over her head. "I am very sorry, Hampton," he said calmly, pleasantly, and finally, "but Catriona cannot marry you."

"So it seems." The marquis sounded very angry. "For how long, may I ask, has this been going on?"

"Catriona and I have loved each other for a

very long time." Edmund's voice sounded very collected. Only Catriona, who could hear his heart hammering against her cheek, had any idea that he was not as composed as he seemed. "However, we were neither of us aware of the other's feelings. We have, as you see, just discovered the truth."

Catriona raised her head. "It's true, Richard," she said. "I've always loved Edmund but I didn't think he loved me back." She looked up at the duke for a fleeting minute and then turned her eyes to Lord Hampton. "I am most terribly sorry," she said. "I have behaved very badly toward you."

"I love you," he said.

"I know." Her eyes shimmered with unshed tears. "I do like you so very much, you see. And I was going to be a good wife to you. At least believe that of me."

He didn't say anything for a minute but stood surveying the two of them. He was very pale, and his cheekbones seemed more prominent than usual under his pallid skin. "I always knew there was someone else," he said unexpectedly to the duke. "But I never dreamed it was you."

"Neither did I," returned Edmund gravely and very gently released Catriona.

"I'll be leaving then," said Lord Hampton. "You'll handle the announcements?"

"Yes." Edmund looked steadily at the marquis. "You *could* have been the man," he said.

"I'd like to think so. But I was too late." He

looked at Catriona. "Good-bye, Kate," he said and left, closing the door behind him.

When Frances and Ian returned to the house, she asked for the duke immediately, but before Hutchins could answer, Edmund's voice came from the door of the morning room. "Here I am." Then he walked into the hall, put his hands under Frances's elbows, and lifted her until her face was on a level with his. "You are a wonderful woman, Frances," he said solemnly and kissed her.

"Wait a minute now!" protested her husband.

Edmund laughed, and his face was bright and boyish. "You can return the compliment and kiss my fiancée," he said, and Ian broke into a grin.

"Congratulations, Burford. So Frances was right." Catriona appeared in the morning room doorway, and Ian shouldered past the duke. "I have permission," he said and kissed her most thoroughly.

"Goodness!" said Catriona, emerging laughing from his embrace. "He's dangerous," she told Frances.

"I keep him on a very tight rein," his wife replied. She smiled at Catriona. "I'm so happy for you, darling." And then the two women embraced.

"What I don't understand," Edmund said later to Ian as they all sat over breakfast, "is how Frances penetrated my secret. I thought I was being very careful."

"Oh, she knew as soon as Talbot told her that Catriona was the only person you ever lost your temper with," Ian replied, lavishly buttering a roll. Edmund looked completely bewildered, and after a minute Ian took pity on him. "The only person who has ever succeeded in putting Frances out of temper," he told his host with a rueful grin, "is me."

Edmund began to laugh. "I see," he said.

"Yes." Ian took a healthy bite of his roll. "In a strangely tortuous way it makes perfect sense."

The butler came back into the breakfast room. "Her Grace is in her boudoir," he told the duke.

"Thank you, Hutchins," Edmund replied and looked at Catriona. "If you've finished eating, Catriona, I think we should go and tell Grandmama."

"Oh, yes," Catriona replied sunnily. "How surprised she will be!"

"There's only one person who will be happier than Grandmama," he said softly as they mounted the stairs together.

"Who is that?" she asked, raising innocent, questioning eyes to his face.

"Me," he answered simply and there, before the fascinated eyes of one of the upstairs maids, he stopped and kissed her again.

EPILOGUE

1827

Our remedies oft in ourselves do lie
Which we ascribe to heaven.
All's Well That Ends Well

Catriona finished burping her daughter and laid the baby gently back in her cradle. Georgianna waved her tiny fists vigorously, and Catriona laughed. The door opened, and the nurse came in. Catriona looked around.

"Oh, good, Mrs. Summers. Georgy's been fed, and I have to go back downstairs. Will you take over, please?"

"Of course, Your Grace." The nurse competently picked up the baby and was murmuring softly to her as Catriona left the room. She looked into the schoolroom, but her sons were not there, so she went down to the drawing room.

Edmund and the boys were with George. Catriona walked in, saw her muddy and wet husband and sons, and said, "You look as if you've had fun."

"It was splendid, Mama." Seven-year-old John turned a glowing if somewhat dirty face toward her. "Papa helped us build a giant dam. I wish you had been there."

"I do too," said Catriona enviously.

"Papa let me hand him the sticks," three-year-old Robin said proudly.

"That's wonderful, darling. I do notice, however, that both of you seem to be dripping on the carpet. I think you'd better run along and change."

"Does that apply to me as well?" her husband asked with amusement.

Catriona smiled at him. He had been buried in some project for almost a month now, and she was delighted to see that he had apparently come up for air. "It's your carpet," she said sunnily. "If you want to drip, drip."

"Yes, Your Grace?" said her butler from behind her.

"Oh, Hutchins. Will you please see that Lord John and Lord Robert get some dry clothes? And an extra big tea, I think."

"Oh, good," said both boys together and went out after the butler, leaving a regrettable trail of muddy footprints. Their mother appeared not to notice.

George looked at the duke and thought of what his wife would say if he ever dared to appear in her drawing room in Edmund's condition. The duke's black hair was disheveled and falling over his forehead, his boots were muddy and so were his knees. But his face looked relaxed and happy. It was impossible to believe, George thought suddenly, that he would be forty next year.

"I just looked in to say hello to George," Edmund was saying to Catriona now. "I really didn't plan to sit and visit until I had changed."

"You look fine," his wife said, and George sighed enviously. Then he cleared his throat. He wanted to get this over with.

"I want you to see this," he said without preamble and handed the marriage lines to the duke.

There was a long silence, and then Edmund looked up. "Where did you find this?" he asked slowly.

"In a book at home." George took a deep breath. "It looks as if someone tried to conceal it."

"But why would anyone do that?" asked Catriona in bewilderment.

Edmund and George exchanged glances.

"It was very good of you to show us this, George," Edmund said very gravely. "Have you told your wife?"

George shook his head. "No," he said unhappily. "I haven't told anyone. I came right here."

Edmund nodded and frowned. "I was only twelve when Diccon died but I remember it quite well. I remember how bewildered everyone was by his constant references to 'Flora.' He was delirious, of course. And then we learned that Flora was a girl he had met in Scotland. And we learned about Catriona." His brow cleared. "Of course Diccon would have married her," he said positively. "He was not the kind to seduce innocent young girls. He must have been coming home to tell us."

"But why didn't *she* say anything?" George asked.

"I'm afraid she thought he had deserted her," Catriona said sadly. "He died, you see, and no one knew of her, so of course she never heard."

"But if they were legally married, he couldn't desert her," George protested.

"The MacIans are all fiercely proud," said Flora's daughter. "She would never hold him to a marriage by force. She wouldn't want him if she had to do that. I'm sure that's why she never told anyone, not even my grandfather, about the marriage. It was he and not my mother who instituted inquiries when he learned she was having a baby."

Edmund's mind appeared to be on another track altogether. "I wonder why he didn't destroy the marriage record completely."

"I don't know," George said heavily. "Perhaps he couldn't bring himself to descend to that level. And there would be a record in Scotland as well."

"True."

"I would appreciate it if someone would let me know what you two were talking about," Catriona said indignantly. "Who is this mysterious 'he'?"

Edmund looked at George.

"My father," George said bitterly. "It must have been he."

"I am afraid it must have been," Edmund said gently.

"But *why*?" appealed Catriona.

"It is a matter of inheritance, sweetheart," said her husband. "Ripon Hall was not entailed, so it would not go to the nearest *male* heir but to the nearest heir." He raised the document he still held in his hands. "Which, it now appears, is you."

"Good heavens," said Catriona. They had all been standing, and now she collapsed into a chair.

"Yes," said George bleakly, "precisely." And he too sat down.

"What shall we do?" Catriona asked after a minute and looked at her husband.

"It is entirely up to you," he said. "Legally Ripon Hall is yours."

Catriona sat up straight. "I don't want Ripon Hall," she said indignantly. "What am I supposed to do? Disinherit George, who has always thought the Hall was rightfully his? Don't be ridiculous." Her mouth looked as severe as it could ever look. "We'd better just tear that up."

Edmund shook his head. "As George pointed out, there will be a record in the church in Scotland. Do you propose that when next we visit the Lochabers we sneak up to Ardnamurchan and destroy that too?"

"No," Catriona looked very somber. "I suppose we can't do that."

"I think your best course," Edmund said briskly, "is to sell Ripon Hall to George."

"Sell it?"

"Of course." George looked grim. "I don't have a lot of ready cash, Edmund. But if you'd give me time . . ."

"Oh, I think you might come up with five guineas, George, don't you?"

"Five guineas?" George looked incredulously at his cousin's face.

"Catriona doesn't want the Hall. And I am very well able to provide for all my children, however many we may have." Edmund looked at Catriona. "What do you say to that bargain?" he asked her.

"Oh, I don't know," she returned mischievously. "I think we might hold out for ten."

George stared at his cousins and then broke into a grin. "Ten it is!" he cried. "Never let it be said that I am a nipcheese."

"Never in my hearing," said Edmund gravely, and Catriona giggled. "Well, as I am afraid to sit down lest I leave mud all over the chair, I think I will excuse myself," the duke continued. "You'll stay to dinner, George?"

"Of course he will," Catriona said immediately.

"Well, since you put it that way," George said with an even bigger grin than before, "thank you, I will."

*   *   *

Later that night, after George had left for home, Catriona and Edmund sat together in the library, talking quietly.

"It was very honorable of George to show us that document," Edmund said. "He must have been greatly tempted simply to tear it up. I was proud of him."

"Well, he grew up with such a model of rectitude for a guardian," Catriona teased. "He had to do the right thing."

"Very funny." They were sitting together on the sofa in front of the fire. His arm was around her and for a brief moment it tightened. "I was proud of you too," he said softly. "Ripon Hall would have tempted a great many people."

Catriona nestled her cheek against his shoulder and closed her eyes. "Not me," she said. "I've already got everything I want."

There was silence except for the sound of wood cracking in the fireplace. Then Edmund said, "Why don't we take the boys for a picnic tomorrow? The weather's turned very fine."

"Marvelous. It will do you good as well. You've been tunneled into this library for almost a month now."

"I've worked out a very interesting formula," he said. "Poor Catriona. I expect I've been a bear to live with."

"Not a bear," she said. "Just—rather absent. It's good to have you back."

His arm loosened, and he turned to look down into her face. "Catriona," he said. "There isn't another woman in the world who would put up with me."

"That's true." She treated him to her most bewitching smile. "Just you remember that, Your Grace."

"I am never, ever, in any danger of forgetting." His face was now very close to hers.

She looked up into his narrowed eyes and sighed. "Oh, Edmund." And then his mouth was on hers. She closed her eyes, sinking into the familiar whirlpool of passion and surrender that his kiss and the promise of what was to follow it always aroused in her.

After a very long minute he raised his head. "Let's go to bed," he said huskily.

"That is an excellent idea," she replied, and hand in hand they went upstairs through the sleeping house.

About the Author

Joan Wolf is a native of New York City who presently resides in Milford, Connecticut, with her husband and two young children. She taught high school English in New York for nine years and took up writing when she retired to rear a family. Her previous books—THE COUNTERFEIT MARRIAGE, A KIND OF HONOR, A LONDON SEASON, A DIFFICULT TRUCE, THE SCOTTISH LORD, MARGARITA, HIS LORDSHIP'S MISTRESS, THE AMERICAN DUCHESS, and LORD RICHARD'S DAUGHTER—are also available in Signet editions.

∅

More Delightful Regency Romances from SIGNET

(045)

☐ **THE ACCESSIBLE AUNT by Vanessa Gray.** (126777—$2.25)
☐ **THE DUKE'S MESSENGER by Vanessa Gray.** (118685—$2.25)
☐ **THE RECKLESS ORPHAN by Vanessa Gray.** (112083—$2.25)
☐ **THE DUTIFUL DAUGHTER by Vanessa Gray.** (090179—$1.75)
☐ **THE WICKED GUARDIAN by Vanessa Gray.** (083903—$1.75)
☐ **THE MYSTERIOUS HEIR by Edith Layton.** (126793—$2.25)
☐ **THE DISDAINFUL MARQUIS by Edith Layton.** (124480—$2.25)
☐ **THE DUKE'S WAGER by Edith Layton.** (120671—$2.25)
☐ **A SUITABLE MATCH by Joy Freeman.** (117735—$2.25)

*Prices slightly higher in Canada

Buy them at your local bookstore or use this convenient coupon for ordering.

THE NEW AMERICAN LIBRARY, INC.,
P.O. Box 999, Bergenfield, New Jersey 07621

Please send me the books I have checked above. I am enclosing $_____
(please add $1.00 to this order to cover postage and handling). Send check
or money order—no cash or C.O.D.'s. Prices and numbers are subject to change
without notice.

Name_____

Address_____

City _____ State _____ Zip Code _____
Allow 4-6 weeks for delivery.
This offer is subject to withdrawal without notice.

Other Regency Romances from SIGNET

(0451)

☐ **THE AMERICAN BRIDE by Megan Daniel.** (124812—$2.25)*

☐ **THE UNLIKELY RIVALS by Megan Daniel.** (110765—$2.25)*

☐ **THE SENSIBLE COURTSHIP by Megan Daniel.**
(117395—$2.25)*

☐ **THE RELUCTANT SUITOR by Megan Daniel.**
(096711—$1.95)*

☐ **AMELIA by Megan Daniel.** (094875—$1.75)*

☐ **THE RUNAWAY BRIDE by Sheila Walsh.** (125142—$2.25)*

☐ **A HIGHLY RESPECTABLE MARRIAGE by Sheila Walsh.**
(118308—$2.25)*

☐ **THE INCOMPARABLE MISS BRADY by Sheila Walsh.**
(092457—$1.75)*

☐ **THE ROSE DOMINO by Sheila Walsh.** (110773—$2.25)*

*Prices slightly higher in Canada

Buy them at your local
bookstore or use coupon
on next page for ordering.

SIGNET Regency Romances You'll Enjoy

(0451

- [ ] **THE MEDDLESOME HEIRESS by Miranda Cameron.**
  (126165—$2.25)▸
- [ ] **A SCANDALOUS BARGAIN by Miranda Cameron.**
  (124499—$2.25)
- [ ] **THE VISCOUNT'S REVENGE by Marion Chesney.**
  (125630—$2.25)▸
- [ ] **THE PERFECT MATCH by Norma Lee Clark.**
  (124839—$2.25)
- [ ] **A MIND OF HER OWN by Anne MacNeill.**
  (124820—$2.25)▸
- [ ] **LADY CHARLOTTE'S RUSE by Judith Harkness.**
  (117387—$2.25)
- [ ] **CONTRARY COUSINS by Judith Harkness.** (110226—$2.25)
- [ ] **THE DETERMINED BACHELOR by Judith Harkness.**
  (096096—$1.95)
- [ ] **THE ADMIRAL'S DAUGHTER by Judith Harkness.**
  (091612—$1.75)

*Prices slightly higher in Canada

Buy them at your local bookstore or use this convenient coupon for ordering.

THE NEW AMERICAN LIBRARY, INC..
P.O. Box 999, Bergenfield, New Jersey 07621

Please send me the books I have checked above. I am enclosing $_____
(please add $1.00 to this order to cover postage and handling). Send check
or money order—no cash or C.O.D.'s. Prices and numbers are subject to change
without notice.

Name_____

Address_____

City _____ State _____ Zip Code _____
Allow 4-6 weeks for delivery.
This offer is subject to withdrawal without notice